Praise for Ruby the Indomitable

"Robin Jansen continues to write captivating books. She is at her best with her multi-layered characterization of Ruby Red. In the 1920s saga, Jansen reels us into heartbreak and healing."

— Kyle Saylors, TV producer and producer of film *Kimjongilla*, theatrically released internationally and nominated for Grand Jury Prize at Sundance, screening at US Capital

"*Ruby the Indomitable* is a poignant story of an abandoned child with an indomitable spirit. The delightful imagery and poetry of written words will propel the reader to the era gone by, bringing a story of hope and survival that will warm even the most jaded hearts."

— Bonnie Calhoun, publisher of *Christian Fiction Online Magazine*

"Robin Jansen has done it again! *Ruby the Indomitable* is a spell-binding tale that will grab you on page one and won't turn you lose until you've read 'The End.' Sadness and grief are superbly balanced with uplifting joy, and when you add this to your keepers shelf, you will feel as though you've met Ruby in person. If I were doling out stars, I'd give Robin all the heavenly stars for this one!"

— Loree Lough, author of over 75 award-winning books

"*Ruby the Indomitable* by Robin Jansen is one of the most exquisitely written, poignant stories I've come across in years. The words sing, even as the tale of Ruby Red breaks your heart and summons you into a deeper, more noble existence. This is the first book by this author and certainly will not be the last."

— Kathi Macias, award winning author of over 40 books

Ruby
the Indomitable

Robin Jansen

ROBIN JANSEN

Family Manor, LLC
Denton, Texas

Ruby the Indomitable by Robin Jansen

Copyright © 2016 Robin Jansen. All rights reserved.

No part of this book may be reproduced, scanned, distributed, or transmitted in any form or by any means, including photocopying, recording, or other electronic or mechanical methods, without the prior written permission of the publisher, except in the case of brief quotations embodied in critical reviews and certain other noncommercial uses permitted by copyright law. Please do not participate in or encourage piracy of copyrighted materials in violation of the author's rights. Purchase only authorized editions.

This is a work of fiction. Names, characters, businesses, places, events and incidents are either the products of the author's imagination or used in a fictitious manner. Any resemblance to actual persons, living or dead, or actual events is purely coincidental.

Books may be purchased by contacting the publisher:

>Family Manor, LLC.
>familymanorpublishing.com
>info@familymanorpublishing.com

Printed in the United States of America

First Edition

ISBN: 978-1-940256-05-4 (print)
ISBN: 978-1-940256-06-1 (ebook)

Colophon

Cover designed by Amy Munoz.

Interior designed by Elise Matthews using Adobe InDesign.

The typefaces are Adobe Garamond Pro for the body text and Gill Sans for chapter titles.

For Kimberly who possesses Ruby's indomitable spirit

For Kalen who wears Frank's traveling shoes

For Matthew who possesses Andy's imagination

For Kingston and Karter who are unspeakable joy

&

Mary for her colors

Because you were there at the very beginning

(and every day since)

Introduction

Homeless children roamed the streets of New York City from the late 1800s through the 1930s. Death and disease were heaped upon poverty and overcrowding, causing thousands of children to be abandoned and left to fend for themselves. Adding to the malaise, boatloads of European immigrants flooded American shores and soon succumbed to the same adversities, leaving thousands of children parentless. Accounts have been written of the Orphan Train that carried white-skinned children out into the heartland of America to find new families, but history is totally silent on what became of the dark-skinned children.

Ruby Red is a fictional character. The setting is based on a true historical event. It's the end of the Orphan Train run in the mid-1920s. This fictional story is told through Ruby Red's eleven-year-old eyes. After Ruby is taken in as a maid, she finds she has little hope of being anything more and makes a risky move by faking insanity. After being expelled from the household, she sneaks onto a train heading west where she meets adventure, encounters peril, and discovers renewed hope.

1
...
New York City, December 1920

Ruby sparkled with beauty like the gem whose name she carried. Her skin was the color of lush earth darkened by the heat of summer's noonday sun. But it wasn't the green of summer. It was the white of winter, and Ruby had no place to call home.

Ruby, medium boned with impish brown eyes and somewhere around eleven years old, stood 57 inches tall. If she could pick her garment, it would be soft and bright to match her spirit. Instead, the fabric coordinated with the drab colors of the kitchen walls which hadn't seen paint in decades. As a child servant, she labored among the potato-filled pots in the spice-scented kitchen. Ruby held her skirt pinched between her fingers, imagining it a party dress, and danced toward the kitchen where a sink of crusted pots and pans waited.

Chilled by early morning winter, she gratefully plunged her arms into the hot, sudsy water clear up to her elbows. Through the window, a haloed sun looked down on her. Its lemony color seeped from the bright cerulean sky. A thin smile spread across her face. This was the best part of the day.

Frozen clusters of frost hung from the trees on the other side of the glass, where sparrows pecked at the edges of stale bread: leftovers from last night's dinner. The blowing snow appeared as flour tossed about on the counter surface whenever Mama Burke made her pies—like now.

From the corner of her eye, she watched the cook, Mama Burke, tied into her feed-sack apron, using singed potholders to move the hot pies from the wood cook stove onto the cooling racks where they were then covered with starched white tea towels.

The warm smell of cinnamon and vanilla with sweet cream caused Ruby's mouth to water. Right about now, she'd be willing to give anything she owned—her writing tablet, her sock doll, or her only pair of shoes—just for one piece of pumpkin pie with a scoop of vanilla ice cream melting down around it on all sides. But she had a feeling she'd get stuck with a slice of mincemeat before the day was done.

"Don't think I can't see you eyeing them pumpkin pies." Mama Burke stood by the gray speckled stove. "We're lucky to be fed from the Mrs. Stone's table. Be thankful for what's left at the end of each day. Hear me, child?"

"Yes, ma'am, *I* hear you, but my tummy ain't paying close attention." Ruby rinsed a pan and set it into the dry sink. "Among other things, you should know I have a lowly opinion of mincemeat pie. Others must feel the same because there's plenty more than one piece left after the meal is done. Baking an unpopular pie seems a waste of time. Your efforts might best be spent baking more pumpkin pie. Everyone likes pumpkin pie"

"You sassing me again, girl?" Laughing caused Mama Burke's belly to quiver. A clump of wiry hair from her tight bun fell across her face. "Ruby girl, you sure have a way with words. Now finish up and stop looking out that window, will you? I saved an extra pie in the pantry just for you. Maybe that'll set a fire under you."

"Pumpkin?" Ruby's dark eyes flashed with hope.

"That's just what it is. Made just the way you like it, with extra cream. When Mrs. Stone and Miss Betsy have their nightcaps on, tucked into bed tonight, I'll give you a fat slice."

"Two fat slices!"

"Two fat slices." She tenderly touched Ruby's cheek.

"It'll be my new favorite time of day."

"Mine, too," Papa Burke, the butler, said, walking into the room.

A satisfied grin spread across Ruby's face.

Ruby could hardly wait until the house was quieted down by sleep. Then, Mama and Papa Burke and Ruby sat together in the kitchen for their daily meal—with pie. Tonight, it'd be with two pieces. Ruby watched Papa Burke tenderly touch Mama Burke's shoulder as he set down the silver tray, filled with the upstairs finished breakfast dishes.

It wasn't the food, but the being together that mattered. Papa Burke with his talk about the wayward world, Mama Burke dabbing her lips with the hem of her apron and silently holding on to each of his words—like a special gift that wouldn't come twice.

Ruby finished the last of the pots and flitted across the room where she used both hands to lift the heavy flour sack from the bin. Leaning down to the bottom, she grabbed her book and tablet before taking her seat at the table where Papa Burke sat sharpening three pencils with his knife. Ruby held the pencil tips together and picked the one with the sharpest point.

"Don't want Mrs. Stone to catch you. Wait till I close the door," Mama Burke whispered with worry in her eyes as she hurried to the door and fearfully looked into hall. Satisfied no one was afoot, she closed the door and stood behind Ruby. "You writing a story?"

Ruby nodded, forming her letters into words and words in sentences.

"What are you writing about?" Mama Burke asked moving back toward the stove.

"I'm writing a story about Miss Betsy's poor behaviors."

"Oh, Ruby, that ain't a good idea." On heavy feet, Mama Burke ran back across the wood floor and jerked the paper from under Ruby's pencil, snapping the point.

"You'll get into all kinds of trouble doing that," Papa Burke quietly scolded. "You could easily find yourself out on the street again, if not all of us alongside you."

Ruby snapped up her head and angrily scrunched her face as Mama Burke crumpled the paper into a ball, opened the stove's fire door, and tossed it in. Flames flickered and immediately consumed the paper.

"Miss Betsy is— sweet. Everyone speaks of her charm." Mama Burke's words weren't intended for truth telling, but to keep peace. Fear of being tossed out of the fine mansion was never far from anyone's thoughts. Ruby's eyes glittered with tears.

"Her charm wears off fast each time she opens her mouth. And Mrs. Stone ain't no better. She has much wealth and little heart."

"Hush, child." Papa Burke rapped his knuckled on the table.

Resigned to acknowledge Mama and Papa Burke's worries as fact, she decided that if she couldn't write a story using honest words, then she'd have to be satisfied drawing her thoughts and memories. Ruby pulled a new page from the tablet and selected the next sharpest pencil which she tapped on the table, making her mind time travel back to the saddest day of her life: the last day she saw her mother.

With long strokes, she drew an upside down V near the top center of the paper. At the peak of the roof, she drew a rectangular shop sign: "BOOKS." It was the first word she learned to read. Below was the square window where she had stood holding her mother's hand, trying to decide which book she wanted for Christmas. With so many to choose from, Ruby made sure to take her time; she needed to pick carefully. This was an important decision. The book would have to last all year. Trying to make a decision, she almost hadn't noticed when her mother's hand slipped from her own. Ruby had spun around just in time to see the back of Mother's red coat disappear through the crowd.

"Mother! Mother!" Ruby called as she ran, forgetting all about books and Christmas. Snow had sprinkled the air before, but now it came thicker—faster like powdered sugar sifted over cookies. Ruby's thin shoes made her slip on the icy sidewalks. Remembering that day caused her heart to beat faster and the images to come quicker. They came in waves, each new one overpowering the last. They tumbled so fast that it was hard keeping up with drawing. The pencil swam over the paper. She sketched faces, snow, and children in the streets. More paper was needed to tell the story properly. A handful was torn from the tablet.

Next, Ruby drew a picture of a five-year-old girl in pigtails standing alone. She formed the girl's lips into a terrified frown. Tears fell from the little girl's eyes to her cheeks and then dripped down, down, pooling around her feet; the air turned the puddle of tears into a frozen pond. Ruby examined her self-portrait. Her work was almost complete.

Ruby laid her head down on the paper, closed her eyes, and tried her best to remember her mother's face so she could draw it now. It was no use. Only the red coat remained in her memory—along with hunger, the fear of the dark sky, and cold seeping through her sweater into the marrow of her bones. Some things were hard to recall while others remained fresh, like the gangs of older, rough children who lived on the streets and were a constant threat.

Salvation had arrived in the form of Mama and Papa Burke. Ruby drew them holding grocery bundles in their arms. Next, she shaded their faces using the side of her pencil. Together, they had searched for her mother, and finally, when all hope was lost, they had taken Ruby home with them and tried to sneak her through the back door along with the groceries.

It had been late. The Mrs. Stone of the house had been watching out the window. She decided to make one of her occasional kitchen visits. With long, full skirts, she swooshed into the kitchen.

"What is this— this creature?" Mrs. Stone stretched a gnarled finger. Afraid she'd be pierced by it, little Ruby back away.

"Sorry we're late, ma'am." Papa Burke nodded then took off his hat and laid it on the counter. "This is Ruby. She got no parents."

Ruby opened her mouth to protest, but Papa Burke shushed her.

"Like so many others, she been abandoned. Look at her. Too young to be on the street alone. She'd be dead by morning if we didn't snatch her away."

"So, Jonathon Burke, you found this stray in the marketplace and thought to bring her home along with the day's groceries?" Mrs. Stone's voice curled. She walked in a wide circle in thick heels around Ruby.

"Yes, ma'am. I mean no, ma'am. I mean, this child is cold and starving. How could I leave her? How could anyone?" Papa Burke's voice was softer, pleading. He never raised his eyes higher than his worn shoes.

"Where's her mother? Has she no father?" Mrs. Stone arched her thinly plucked brows.

"We don't know where they is. Couldn't find them." Mama Burke held up her hands.

"By the time the gas street lamps were lit, we were bone cold and tired from looking. We hitched a ride back in a wagon." Papa Burke's eyes remained on his shoes.

"So I saw out the front windows while waiting for my supper." Mrs. Stone looked closely at Ruby, checking inside her ears and peering into her mouth. "This child is filthy. Her teeth need cleaning, and her hair is tangled into knots. I hope she hasn't acquired lice. Speak to me girl, where is your mother and father?"

Glad she could now say something, she decided to follow Papa Burke's cue. Ruby now took her turn while looking down at her scuffed shoes. "Never had a father. Only my mother. I think she got herself quite lost today."

"You think she's lost? *What?*"

"She's lost from me." Ruby drew back from the displeased look on Mrs. Stone' face. Ruby figured she had answered wrong and there was now trouble in the house because of it. Things never went well again when started out badly.

"When speaking to me, finish all your sentences with ma'am or Mrs. Stone! Do you hear me, *girl?*" Mrs. Stone's look of reserve slipped off her face just a bit.

"Yes, ma'am-Mrs.-Stone." Fear rising faster than ice in a glass of water, Ruby tugged at her braids and found they had come undone during the rush of the day. Then, Ruby noticed a blonde-headed girl about her age peeking out from around Mrs. Stone's skirts. Ruby smiled, hoping to make a friend. Miss Betsy returned her greeting by sticking out her tongue that was streaked red from the striped candy cane she held.

"Excuse me, Mrs. Stone," Papa Burke politely began. "It is Christian charity to forgive this orphan of her rudeness. It's obvious she wasn't brought up proper like Miss Betsy. But it's Christmastime, and it's cold outside."

"I don't need a reminder of the time of year, nor of my Christian duty!" Mrs. Stone huffed and licked her persimmon-colored lips thoughtfully.

"Perhaps she can stay, Mother—if she works." Betsy waved her candy beneath her mother's flabby chin.

"She looks too small to be much help. How old are you?"

"Five, Mrs. Stone, ma'am," Ruby barely whispered.

"There's plenty she can do, Mama."

"You do like your bed sheets daily washed and pressed." Mrs. Stone said.

"I do. And I like all my toys put away in their place."

"And you love to eat ice cream in bed at all hours!" Mrs. Stone chided.

"I'm sure there are other things for her to do. I know—I shall make a list!" Betsy smiled mischievously.

"What a good idea, my dearest. No charity goes unrewarded in this household." She thinly smiled.

Ruby eyed the door, wondering how fast she could make it back onto the street without anyone catching her. Just as she geared up to find out, Papa Burke laid a calming hand on her shoulder. It held her in place for a single heartbeat.

"There's always potatoes that need peeling and cake batter that needs stirring, not to mention a turkey that needs basting here in the kitchen with Mrs. Burke. Come summer, there'll be garden weeding." Papa Burke patted the waif's head. "She'll be a great help to both of us. It's good to teach them in the ways of taking care of the household when they're young like this. Ruby's small now, but she'll grow and take on more and more work. Under your guidance, she'll become a fine servant."

"Well, you are getting on in years. Perhaps it's time to look for youthful help." Mrs. Stone waved her hand as though she was done with them. Ruby was quite sure there was going to be a lot more work involved than she could envision. But after all that food talk, she gave it little thought. Work for food and a bed. It was worth the winter trade.

She would stay just until spring melted off the snow and the air cleared of cold. Then she'd get back to the business of finding her lost mother.

Ruby stayed.

Miss Betsy made lists.

Mrs. Stone ensured Ruby did them.

And Ruby loved her new home with Mama and Papa Burke.

She was without one for a while until Mama and Papa Burke came along and let her use theirs for about six years. The older servants slept in the supply room off the kitchen while Ruby slept on a cot under the hallway eaves between their bedroom and the kitchen. As long as the Burkes lived there, Ruby was welcome. In just a few weeks, it was as though she had been there forever, but one thing nagged at her: the memory of her mother. Never would she forget. Never. Ruby fell asleep each night for the next six years and dreamed that her mother came knocking on the door of this house, selling books. When the door opened, she'd see Ruby standing right there and say, "There you are, Ruby! I been looking all over for you!"

2
...
Christmas Eve, 1920

Eleven-year-old Ruby shivered with fear. With achy arms, she balanced the heavy silver tray down the long staircase from Miss Betsy's room. If she dropped her load, the whole house would come running to see what she had done this time.

Safety was reaching the kitchen in one piece, where Mama and Papa Burke were still up preparing tomorrow's Christmas Day meal.

Anxiously watching her step and not wanting to lose control of the tray, Ruby steeled her will not to fall. Mrs. Stone would be most upset with any mess that wound up on her fancy carpet that recently arrived from France. Picturing vanilla ice cream with chocolate syrup spread out like a picnic without plates caused Ruby's throat to go dry with dread. At last, she reached the bottom of the landing and let out a relieved breath.

Just as she turned into the hallway leading directly to the kitchen, Ruby noticed the parlor doors at the front of the house had been left open. That room was only used for two occasions: to entertain important guests and for Christmas, when the parlor was referred to as the Christmas Room. On neither occasion was Ruby allowed entrance, and that niggled at her.

No one was in sight. This part of the house was deserted and still. One quick peek wouldn't hurt. She set down the tray, assuring herself it would be all right for her to close the doors. It was the right thing to do. As she approached, the Christmas Room jumped to life. The double doors became arms gesturing her inside. She teetered at the threshold of the forbidden room. The warm glow of the room radiated on Ruby's flushed face.

There was no fairy tale Santa to see. It was better—the room blazed with magic. The exquisitely decorated Christmas tree welcomed her and caused her worn body to blossom with renewed energy. The new electric lights shined from every branch, rendering her powerless to do anything but step even closer. Through no fault of her own, the pungent odor of the blue spruce drew her across the large room to where it reached the ten-foot ceiling. Hundreds of colored glass ornaments wrapped her in their spell. Not only did they reflect light around the walls of the room, but they also illuminated Ruby. A pattern of diamonds dotted her black maid's dress. Her jaw slacked for she knew right then that this was an enchanted room.

The striped peppermint candy canes hung like ladies' earrings on every branch. She'd seen Miss Betsy lick them until they dissolved into thin, brittle lines. Ruby wanted to have a taste. Once would be enough. Here they hung, and here she stood. Perhaps she'd sneak one from the back of the tree, near the wall, where no one would ever notice it missing. Mouth watering with anticipation, Ruby stood on her toes and unhooked a cane, quickly slipping it into the pocket of her apron. No one saw. No one knew. If she was careful, she'd try to make it last until springtime.

Beads of paper-thin mercury were strung from the shining star and wound around and around the tree down to where wrapped packages lay neatly stacked. They wooed her to remain there, to touch them. She gave in and carefully stroked a bell ornament. The sound of the delicate ring captured Ruby, but the sharp sting of pine needles was so unexpected that she pulled her hand quickly back, breaking the thread that held the bell in place. Ruby looked down to see the bell in pieces lying at her feet. Frightened over the sharp reprimand she'd surely receive, she picked up each broken piece, every shaving of glass, and quickly tossed it all into the fireplace embers.

Now that her blunder was buried, she lowered herself to a sitting position on the soft, thick carpet directly under the tree. For the first time, she felt complete, as if she belonged in this room. Yawning, she felt a bit sleepy and lay on her back where she looked up through the center at the splendor: the scent of the blue spruce branches, the new electric lights, the reflecting glass balls, and the glory of Christmas. Immersed in pure joy, it flooded her head and heart and went clear down to her curled toes. This was the most perfect moment in her life. Good things were about to come her way.

And then, something even more wonderful caught her attention.

Mere inches away, a porcelain doll peeked out from between presents. The dress was elegant and felt slick like pudding. But it was her hair color that hypnotized Ruby. It was red, the same shade as the blush of sky the sun painted while it was still low on the horizon. The same shade as her mother's coat as she disappeared through the throngs of people so many Christmases ago.

Ruby held up the doll and tipped it back and forth watching as its glass eyes open and then clunk closed. Ruby folded the figure into her arms and began singing a lullaby. Just as she finished, there came a terrible scream. She wheeled toward the door.

There stood Miss Betsy. "Thief! Thief!" Betsy's curls shook every which way about her head. She kept pointing and screaming, "That doll is for *me*! Mama! Help, Mama! Ruby is stealing all my presents!"

Ruby scrunched her face at Betsy, thinking she was a pretty picture without meaning—no kindness—a picture no one wanted to see.

The sounds of Mrs. Stone' feet were heavy on the stairs, and soon she came rushing into the room with her velvety night robe flung open, the untied sash flying. Right behind came the Burkes.

"Ruby! What are in the world are you doing?" Mrs. Stone demanded an answer. The sheer sight of her face all puffed was enough to make anyone faint with utter fright. Ruby felt her blood turn cold but refused to show fear.

Ruby crawled from beneath the tree and jumped to her feet. She did her best to hide the doll in the folds of her skirt. "Nothing, Mrs. Stone."

"She is stealing is what she is doing!" screamed Betsy.

"You were to get the tray and come straight to the kitchen," Mama Burke snapped.

Ruby remained motionless.

Papa Burke exchanged a look with Mrs. Stone.

Mrs. Stone pointed. "It seems we have a servant who not only does not know her place, but is also a thief!"

"I ain't a thief. I was just looking at the lights and ornaments. It's all so very beautiful." The rooms enchantment quickly faded as Ruby trembled.

Papa Burke waved Ruby to him. Once she complied, he carefully removed the doll from her and returned it to his employer.

"I— I'm so sorry, Mrs. Stone, ma'am. I was only admiring."

"That is an Armand Marseille all the way from Germany. A very expensive doll. Not only could you have broken it, but you have spoiled Betsy's surprise gift," Mrs. Stone snapped.

Right on cue, Betsy began to cry.

"It's okay, my dear child. Here is your dolly. Safe and sound in your arms." Mrs. Stone placed the toy into Miss Betsy's outstretched hands. "When employees steal, I have no other recourse but to send them away."

"Please, Mrs. Stone. She's just a child mesmerized by a toy. Please show God's mercy," Papa Burke pleaded. "It's Christmastime."

"I know what time of the year it is, Mr. Burke." She heaved a heavy sigh. "Very well. Being the charitable Christian that I am, I will show mercy—for now. Meanwhile, it would be best—for all concerned for this child—that she stay out of the main part of the house. I do not wish to see Ruby's face and be reminded of this horrific incident during the season of our beloved Christ's birth. Later, I will decide what to do."

Without another word, everyone went to bed: Miss Betsy, with her Armand Marseille doll, and Mrs. Stone climbed the long polished staircase to the second floor where silk curtains draped the large windows. The Burkes went to their small room just off the kitchen, and Ruby went to her bed with her sock doll under the eaves of the servants' quarters. Starring at the ceiling, Ruby pondered over the tree and the lights and the glass ornaments. The doll. About silly Betsy. How puffed out the Mrs. Stone's face got. How upset Papa and Mama Burke were. Yet if she lived to be 100 years old, she'd never again see such a sight as that Christmas Room. It was worth all the yelling. Of course, Ruby knew she almost lost her home to the cold snow of winter, but Papa Burke saved her—again. She'd make up for her mistake somehow and lie low. Reaching under the covers, she pulled out her candy cane. She broke off a little piece and stuck the rest back under her mattress. Lying back, she closed her eyes. She slipped the small piece into her mouth, then smiled. Yes, the peppermint was as delightful as she had imagined.

3

New Year's Day, 1921

Mama Burke whipped fresh eggs for scrambling. Papa Burke thoughtfully buttered warm biscuits, and Ruby held her sock doll. A week past the Christmas incident, Ruby was pretty sure it'd be a while until she tasted pumpkin pie. At least she hadn't been sent away.

"I found you something you might like to read." Papa Burke slid a comic book across the table to Ruby.

"Oh boy! Where did you get it?" Ruby turned the pages as if they were gilded.

"Found it in the trash bin."

"Thank you, Papa Burke." Ruby went right to reading.

Mama Burke scooped the eggs from the frying pan and shook them onto the plates with a large wood spoon.

"What's an orphan, Papa Burke?"

"An orphan is someone who doesn't have a mama or a papa."

"Like you," Mama Burke said.

"I ain't no orphan. I have you. And I have a mother; I just haven't found her yet." Ruby continued reading. "It says here that Orphan Annie was a— what's this word?"

Papa Burke set down his fork to dig out reading eyeglasses from his pocket and placed them onto his nose. "Pathetic waif."

"What's a pathetic waif?"

"Someone who's sad and useless."

"Like Miss Betsy." Ruby kept on reading.

"Hurry and eat. We got work to do." Mama Burke placed their breakfast plates on the table.

"It also says Orphan Annie has an indom— indom— What's that word?"

"Indomitable spirit." Papa Burke read over her shoulder. "I think it means she has strength of mind. Courage. Whatever comes her way, she comes out on top."

"That's me; I got an indomitable spirit, too!"

"That you do, child! You most certainly do!" Papa Burke's laugh soon turned into a choking cough.

"You feeling okay, Papa Burke?" Ruby moved his tea closer. "Here, take a drink."

"Good morning." Mrs. Stone stood at the doorway and sucked the happiness right out of the room.

Ruby swiftly covered her comic book over with a napkin.

Mama and Papa Burke stood.

"What do you need, Mrs. Stone?" Papa Burke asked, trying to catch his breath.

"Just saying, 'good morning.'" Mrs. Stone slowly peered about the room.

Ruby carefully inspected the woman's expression, not understanding the sudden interest of Mrs. Stone's entry into a room she hadn't stepped foot in since apple-picking time.

Mrs. Stone opened cupboard doors and checked the contents of the shelves.

Papa Burke watched, taking one sip and then another of tea. "All the supplies are there, just as you ordered, Mrs. Stone. The inventory is on the clipboard."

Mrs. Stone stood with hands on her hips. And then her gaze fell upon the Hoosier cabinet—the hiding place for Ruby's lessons. Ruby watched with guarded eyes, tucking her breath in tight; too afraid to take another breath of air. Servants were only allowed to read lists of chores—nothing more. Mrs. Stone walked to the cabinet on heavy feet and tipped down the flour bin. What followed was three full minutes of torment. Ruby examined her fingernails. Papa Burke wiped his brow. Mama Burke sat and jiggled her legs.

"Is there anything I can help you find, Mrs. Stone?" Papa Burke calmly asked.

"Everything seems to be here. By the way, when coming down the hall, I distinctly heard Ruby reading."

Mama Burke, Papa Burke, and Ruby froze in place, like pictures on a page.

Miss Betsy skipped into the room. Her face was a mixture of anger and satisfaction. "Ruby can't read."

"I can so!" Ruby's knee-jerk reaction was to defend herself, which she knew immediately was a mistake. The words tumbled before anyone could draw a breath. "A comic book is all." She held it up.

"It's only intended for the fire." Papa Burke nudged Ruby with his knee.

Mrs. Stone eyed Ruby up one side and down the other—and her inspection reaffirmed that she didn't like her, no, not one bit. Then she drew her shawl up around her neck and walked straight across the room. "Intended for the fire, eh?" she spoke without kindness.

Ruby kept her head lowered, holding tightly onto her book.

"The room feels chilly to me. It should really be warmer. Burn the comic book, Ruby." Mrs. Stone impatiently tapped the toe of her shoe against the hickory wood floor.

Ruby refused to move. Found in the trash, plucked out by Papa Burke, the comic rightly belonged to her now. Fear turned to anger, and she stared at an old stain on the tablecloth, hoping something would happen to make the moment pass and get everyone's mind off her reading.

"You heard her, Ruby. Put it in the stove," Papa Burke commanded.

She had to obey the tone of his voice.

Ruby jumped up from the table, making the plates rattle. She marched over to the stove, moved one of the cast iron lids to the side with the lifter, and then dropped the book into the canister. Flames rose higher and licked the sides of the book. Finally, the book disappeared completely. All Ruby could think about was how her written words about Miss Betsy got burned up and now poor Orphan Annie was up in flames, too. This was tragedy of horrific proportions.

Mrs. Stone placed her hands together. "It already feels warmer," she mused in a most satisfied manner and began to leave the room.

Papa Burke groaned. Ruby turned to see him tug at the collar on his white button-down shirt, his face taking on a distant look before he dropped his fork.

"Papa Burke?" Ruby ran to him and touched his sleeve, noticing a swipe of butter on his cuff.

As if he was battling an invisible enemy Papa Burke's hand came up and knocked the eyeglasses off his face. His eyes rolled back into his head until there was only white left to see. He slid off the left side of his chair and crumpled to the floor. Ruby wet a rag at the sink pump and then knelt beside him, wiping his forehead while the doctor was called.

Miss Betsy began her high pitched screams.

"Quiet down, will you?" Ruby asked. "Your charm's melting away."

Miss Betsy flew to her mother. "Ruby needs a whipping."

Mrs. Stone remained silent as tears swept her eyes. The unexpected sight of compassion caught Ruby by surprise.

"Sweet Papa Burke. It's probably just indigestion caused by recent bad news. Take deep breaths now so I know you're fine." Ruby brushed back his tight gray curls. "I'm sorry I've caused you misery. Breathe easy. I'll do better. I promise."

"Ruby," Papa Burke puffed, "you never brought one ounce of misery. Only many pounds of joy." His eyes closed, and his body jerked once, then became unnaturally still.

The doctor came through the back door and stood for several minutes staring at the man sprawled out on the ground with Ruby motionless, draped over him, softly crying. "I can't lose you. I need you. Say you'll be okay, Papa Burke. My papa."

"Come, Ruby—let the doctor do his work." The Mrs.

Stone stood erectly next to Miss Betsy, who by now had found solace by licking her candy cane.

Reluctantly, Ruby got to her feet. She went directly into Mama Burke's arms and laid her head on Mama Burke's shoulder.

The doctor listened to Papa Burke's heart and then checked his pulse. "He has crossed over." *Crossed over* was a nice way of saying he had left his body and was floating around somewhere else. Mama Burke hurried to the window and opened it. "I'm setting his spirit free."

"Papa Burke! No! No! No!" Ruby screamed. "Come back to me, Papa Burke! Take me with you!"

"Go to your room, Ruby. He needs to be taken away in peace," Mrs. Stone said.

Ruby took a final look at Papa Burke, who seemed to be napping, not passing. She knelt beside the older man for the very last time. "I love you, Papa Burke." There on the floor beside him were his eyeglasses, frames bent, the lenses shattered. She slipped them into her pocket before running from the kitchen and into the bedroom where she flung herself onto his side of the bed.

Not even exhaustion quelled her sobs. Each time she fell into slumber, she awakened with a jolt and started up her weeping all over. Mama Burke had nothing to offer Ruby in the way of comfort. It was like all joy had dropped out of the woman, leaving a walking shell, just going through the movement of breathing until her own passing.

Days later, Jonathon Burke's body was placed into the ground at the pauper's cemetery. Poor black church people gave money for the plot and the box. Ruby pulled her hair down over her forehead so no one could see her bloodshot, swollen eyes. About a dozen mourners stood around the gravesite singing all at once so the tune sounded like a bevy of angels taking wing heavenward. Bible in hand, the preacher spoke at full volume. He talked to Jesus, trying to be heard above the singing voices. Ruby figured there wasn't a person there who clearly heard a word he had to say, except for the amening part which took twice as long as the song. When it was time to go, Ruby's heart sped up a bit. She didn't want to leave Papa Burke out in the cold by himself. The grave was yet unmarked, and talk was it would remain that way due to lack of money.

That night, Ruby was awakened by a terrible scream coming from the direction of Mama Burke's room. Frightened, Ruby held her sock doll to her and swallowed hard. She found Mama Burke sitting up in bed. The streetlight lit the room just enough to leave curious shadows.

"Ruby girl, did you see him, too?" Mama Burke's eyes were wide as her fried eggs.

Ruby looked about the room. "See who?"

Mama Burke's face crumbled. She wept into her hands. "Papa. Papa Burke was here."

Ruby sat at the edge of the bed. "Papa Burke has crossed. He ain't here no more."

"Oh, but he was here. Seems he wants to keep an eye on us. He don't trust that Mrs. Stone. No not a bit, so his ghost remains."

Feeling a sudden shot of chills, Ruby looked around the room, tingling with the thought of Papa Burke still being about the place. "Did he have any words about Miss Betsy?"

"Had no words to say about anyone. Just stood over there by the window shade."

Goosebumps covered Roby's arms.

"His body might be in his grave, but his ghost is here with us, Ruby girl."

A few days later, just as Ruby was adjusting to Papa Burke being home again in spirit, Mrs. Stone had reached a decision. "It's time for Ruby to live elsewhere."

Ruby looked up from the scrub pots. "Mrs. Stone, I've stayed out of the front part of the house just like you said. I work real hard here in the kitchen. Tonight, I'm making fresh rolls that will melt in your mouth."

"My mind is made up."

"But she got nowhere to live." Mama Burke moved toward Ruby.

"Just this morning, I hired a young butler who will give us many years of service. He also has a wife who will take care of the second floor. Mrs. Burke, you may continue with your duties in the kitchen."

"What about Ruby?"

"What about her? For six years, I have allowed Ruby to stay, living off the bounty of this home and my charity. If you open your mouth one more time, Mrs. Burke, you can pack your things and go with her as well. These are hard days, and I can easily replace you with so many out of work."

Mama Burke hung her head.

"Good choice. At your late age, you wouldn't find work and would be dead on the street within days." Mrs. Stone twirled in her skirts right out of the room.

The following morning, Ruby dressed in Miss Betsy's

outgrown coat that had been plucked from the pile meant for the Salvation Army. Ruby figured with Papa Burke now a ghost and Mama Burke's home threatened, there wasn't anyone to defend her. Feeling sorry for oneself, or wishing for something that could never be, was a waste of time. Mama Burke confirmed it when she kissed her goodbye. "Just as things turned out for Orphan Annie, things will turn out for you, too."

"But the book got burned up. I never read the end. I don't know what happens."

Mama Burke remained motionless for a moment, looking into the distance. Then, as though arriving at the answer she might have gotten from Papa Burke, she tilted up Ruby's chin to look at her. Mama Burke's voice came out strained. "She found herself a home. You will, too."

Resisting her exile, Ruby flung her arms around Mama Burke's neck. Life was suddenly so unfair. First, her mother got lost. Then, the only papa she had ever known crossed over. And now, she was losing Mama Burke. Ruby considered it bad enough being orphaned, but even worse to be discarded.

"I don't want to leave you, Mama Burke."

Mama Burke handed Ruby's rag doll to her. "Here, keep this with you."

Ruby's eyes were so filled with water, she could hardly see. "I want to tell Papa Burke's ghost goodbye."

"He already knows. I love you, Ruby girl."

Ruby held on to Mama Burke as tightly as she could. Just as she was about to tell Mama Burke she loved her, too, she was interrupted by the firm hand of Mrs. Stone on her shoulder, shuffling her toward the open door. Feeling her body break into a chill, Ruby pulled her gaze from the street long enough to see Mama Burke wiping back tears.

Ruby stood outside on the top step and did her best to appear cheerful as she waved goodbye to Mrs. Stone who looked at her without expression, pulled the rag doll from her arms, and shut the walnut door. Ruby looked about deciding which direction to walk. The streets were filled with snow drifts, and her shoes would fill with it, too, in no time at all. As she carefully navigated down the steps onto the sidewalk, there came a tapping at the front window. Hopeful it was Mrs. Stone changing her mind, Ruby looked, only to see Miss Betsy holding up the red headed China doll, along with the sock doll, and sucking on a candy cane.

Ruby narrowed her brow. "You may have things, but I have an indomitable spirit!"

She pulled the coat collar up around her ears, and with her head held high—mimicking Mrs. Stone posture—Ruby walked tall down the avenue lined with mansions. Tears stung on her face, rubbing her cheeks raw, but she'd never let anyone in that mansion see them.

4
...

Ruby walked for what seemed like miles.

Cold and afraid, she sat on a snowy bench near the tenements, far from the lovely street she once thought of as home. Had she and her mother lived here? It was hard to recall. Just like that, it occurred to Ruby that the misguided decision of Mrs. Stone was actually her golden opportunity. The recent turn of events concerning employment freed up her time to look for her mother again. Of course, it would help to remember what she looked like since years separated them one from the other. Reality and memory could be enemies.

Ruby was older now. More confident about finding her. Getting to her feet, she brushed snow off her backside and set out to find the bookstore. Maybe her mother would be there today looking through the window at the books again. She'd recognize her daughter straightaway. "Ruby, there you are! I came back here to find you! And here you are today, my post-Christmas miracle! My, how tall you've grown!"

Feeling giddy with joy, Ruby climbed over the snowdrifts, heading further into the city where the shops were located. After searching for a while, she couldn't find the bookstore. Not only were Ruby's hands freezing, but so were her legs. Her teeth chattered, and there was the ache in her belly that could only be satisfied with food. Ruby pulled the candy cane from her pocket and shoved the rest into her mouth. It didn't do a bit of good in staving off her hunger.

Soon she found herself in the marketplace, hoping to catch a glimpse of Mama Burke shopping for daily groceries. Certainly, she'd give her food. As she jutted between shoppers, Ruby spotted a boy, a little taller than she, running off with a loaf of bread tucked under his coat. The baker hadn't noticed.

If she took food, she needed to be clever not to be seen. Ruby watched vendors, waiting for them to look away from their goods. It wasn't long before she saw her chance. The dairyman walked back into his shop.

Eyeing a wedge of cheese, she reached for it just as she heard sharp voices. There, near the curve of the street, two men argued over a grocery bill. The larger man shoved the smaller man. As he walked off, he dropped his leather glove. Worthy of the reward of a few coins, Ruby picked it up from the snow bank. "Here, sir!" she called to him waving the glove in the air. The man stopped and snatched the glove. No coins were dropped into her chafed hand, no nod of the head was given, not even a perfunctory "Thank you." He simply continued on his way without a backwards glance.

Disappointed, Ruby let out a puffy-cheeked sigh. With her next step, she slipped, and down she went. Ruby didn't move a toe but lay still, looking up at the sky and watching as faces drifted past. No one stopped to help. No one asked if she was hurt. No one paid any attention at all; they walked past as if she were not even there. "I sure could use a visit from you, Papa Burke."

An idea bubbled in Ruby's head. Perhaps, without warning, she had frozen to death and crossed over, just like Papa Burke. It was time to find out. Ruby decided to ask someone a rude question. If answered, she lived. If they went on their way, then she truly had crossed over, too. What mischief she could make! Right off, she'd go back to the mansion and hide that red headed doll where no one could find her. How amusing to watch everyone frantically hunt for it as dear, blue-eyed Betsy screamed.

The sugary desserts in the pantry would be all hers to gorge on. She'd even move around the furniture at night in the forbidden front parlor. When guests arrived, she'd break their teacups and listen to them scream. Then she'd whisper bloodcurdling words into the ear of the sleeping Mrs. Stone until she sat up in bed and shrieked the nightcap right off her head. Yes, Ruby would forever be a nuisance; it's the least she could do to repay them for tossing her out in the freezing winter in a coat that was much too small.

Ah, there up ahead was a woman with a fur coat snugly pulled about her overfed figure. She carried a large wicker basket in her hand. Moving between outdoor shops as though her energy was in short supply, the woman stopped to inspect Brussels sprouts. A few dozen were carefully chosen. When she counted out her coins to the vendor one by one, he scooped the vegetables into a small bag and then set it next to a cut of meat wrapped in butcher paper down inside her basket. The woman's young son held onto a pleat in her skirt that stuck out from the fold of her coat. Squinting eyes in thought, Ruby finally decided they'd be a good pair to test out her suspicions.

"There's sad news to tell. I just saw the butcher picking his nose, and now you're buying his fat, green buggers for dinner. Yum!" Ruby crossed her eyes, pulled on her earlobes, and stuck out her tongue.

"You little beast!" The lady dumped the Brussel sprouts onto the sidewalk. Rekindling her energy, she grabbed her child's wrist and hurried away.

Being visible turned out to be the second disappointment of the day, but at least she now had something to eat. She scrambled to pick up each sprout depositing them into her pocket.

"Apples, oranges, bananas!" hollered a man with a belly that fell over his belt like melting ice cream. "Get your fresh fruit!" In one hand he held up a long knife ready to strike the orange lying on a table. With one heavy stroke, he sliced through the sphere and a section was handed to an elderly man to sample, but when he bit into it, juice ran down his front staining his silk jacket. Livid, the gentleman tossed it to the ground. Ruby scampered for it and shoved it up her sleeve to eat later. Pilfering was wrong, but in her delirium of hunger, she ignored the sin and hooked a banana from a wooden crate.

The wind swirled snow as Ruby ran down the street nearly colliding with a butcher who tossed sawdust on the icy sidewalk to stop people from falling. The white apron tied about his waist was splashed with red. There above her head, waving in the winter wind, were a dozen or more feathery chickens hanging limply from hooks, mouths gaped open, eyes lifelessly staring at her. Ruby covered her mouth from the raucous odor of drained poultry blood. The sticky drippings of the recently slaughtered fouls stuck to the soles of her shoes. Her stomach lurched.

Ruby hurried from the market's rank smells. Once her nostrils had sufficiently cleared, she squatted down on an abandoned wheel on the open street. Now her hands trembled from hunger as she jiggled the orange from her sleeve. The promise of both the orange and banana was tantalizing.

Just as she parted her chapped lips to eat, she felt a whack against the back of her head, sending her down on all fours onto the icy avenue. The orange section was jerked away. A chill of fear waved across her body as she looked up to see the biggest, meanest street boy of all.

"My name's Louie. This is my territory! You ain't allowed."

A full head taller than she and arms as wide as a cinder block, Louie filled her with fear. Tangling with him might be worse than freezing to death. If Ruby was going to survive, she could only count on herself. Struggling to her feet, Ruby waved her arms about trying to appear larger and less helpless. "Give the orange back!" she held out her hand and the banana slipped out.

The well-muscled teen leaned into her face and laughed as he took that, too. Soon, he was gone from sight. The only thing he left behind was the weapon. She stuck the kindling in her right pocket alongside of the Brussels sprouts. Ruby rubbed her head, and again people walked around her. No, she wasn't invisible. She was insignificant. Puckering her face, she fought back more tears that stung like fire.

Her thin shoes became heavy with snow. She walked until she felt she might drop from exhaustion. The cold chafed the exposed skin of her legs, face, and hands. The coat wasn't much good against the drop in temperature. By then, it was nightfall, and all she could think about was her small, warm bed and the taste of pumpkin pie and hot tea to warm her insides. The thought crossed her mind to return to the Mrs. Stone and beg for mercy. If turned away, she'd duck around the side of the house to find a spot in the carriage house out of the wind, but first she needed a place to rest.

Across the street stood an empty carriage. Ruby looked around to make sure no one saw her climb inside. To her delight, there was a wool blanket left folded on the seat. She wrapped it around herself, and her breaths came in ragged gasps. She removed a few Brussels sprouts from her pocket to nibble. They were hard to chew. Overcome with exhaustion, Ruby lay down, and mind became dazed with the tribulations of the day. She was certain she'd be a goner by sunrise.

5

Slowly, Ruby opened her eyes.

Expecting to see the usual ceiling cracks overhead, she was surprised to see her breath as a frosty maze against a curtain of dark fabric. For a moment, she forgot where she was. Panic rose in her chest thinking she was encased in a tomb. Fearing she had been buried, Ruby jolted straight up, screaming. A rush of memories washed over her. Papa Burke was dead, turned ghost. Mrs. Stone sent her away while Mama Burke remained resigned.

Ruby pushed aside the wool blanket. There was a terrible ache in her bones from sleeping all night curled tightly into a ball. Slowly, she unfurled her arms and legs while looking out the window at the start of another day. Already, people were on the street.

The hollow pain in her empty stomach was dreadful. Her mouth watered for Mama Burke's eggs and bacon. How she wished she were sitting at the table between Mama and Papa Burke reading her comic book in the warmth of the kitchen. If only she could turn back time, she would never write another bad word about Miss Betsy. Never would she allow the magical powers of the Christmas Room do her in again. But there was no turning back the hands on a clock. Time ticked forward. As she nibbled on another Brussels sprout, all that mattered was today, which meant stealing food and finding a safe place to sleep. What were the chances of finding another unlocked carriage tonight? One thing was constant: worry.

Ruby opened the carriage door and looked both ways before hopping out onto the ice-slick street. She teetered gingerly along behind house servants on their way to the market, keeping an eye out for Mama Burke.

She walked a few blocks to Canal Street where carts and wooden bins brimmed with food. Shoppers haggled over prices with the vendors. Ruby watched for several minutes, hoping to make her move. A man shoveling the sidewalk suddenly stopped and looked both ways before going back inside his shop. A butcher was busy with a woman who wore a purple plume in her hat.

Seeing her chance, Ruby grabbed a smoked fish from a bin. It was time to gulp down her catch, but today she'd be alert, watching for danger. Ruby took the alleyway behind a building where wash was hung out on long clotheslines, looking rather festive. It was perfect; no one could see it from the street. Here, she'd be safe for a little while. There was a place to sit with the garbage cans on one side and stacks of timber boxes on the other.

Going from one metal trashcan to the next, she finally spied a nice piece of hard bread with a leftover piece of meat near the crust that had been missed. What luck! Just out of reach, Ruby stood on the tips of her shoes and leaned in to get it. As she flicked coffee grounds to the side, a furry head with two eyes and a nose popped up. A giant rat with a long hairless tail was ready for battle.

Shrieking, Ruby fell backwards into a pile of rubbish where she touched something hard and cold. From clots of refuse, she pulled out a small clear bottle meant for canning. Ruby examined it carefully turning it over and over in her hand. No chips nor hairline cracks and the lid still intact. Unscrewing the top, she washed the container off with snow. After drying both inside and out with the hem of her dress, she slid it into the left coat pocket.

The delicious belly filling, pain relieving food was all she could think about. Ruby pulled back the fish skin, allowing it to fall into her lap as she gobbled the tender meat in three huge bites. Oil squirted out the sides of her mouth, so she ran her tongue around her lips to catch every drop. She closed her eyes and chewed slowly, savoring the flavor.

Something small crept up a bare leg and into the folds of her dress. Ruby opened her eyes in time to see it run headlong into the fish skins. In her surprise, she jumped, causing it to disappear into an empty carton. Tilting the edge, she saw the insect. To her delight, the small red jewel was alive. Just like her, it survived in the dead of winter.

Ruby took the jar from her pocket and unscrewed the lid, while keeping an eye on the insect. Once her hand was closed over the top of the carton to block any last minute escape, she tipped the insect into the jar, careful not to injure the prize. The insect was deep red in color with spiny legs and two lovely fans made his wings. Next she scooped up a bit of fish skin and dropped that into the bottom of the jar along with a Brussels sprout. She screwed the tin lid back on tight. With a rusty nail, she punched several holes into the lid. She peered lovingly at her captured friend. At first, the creature appeared stunned, but slowly the long antennas began to drum against the glass.

"You can trust me to keep you safe and warm and to feed you. My name's Ruby. What's your name?" Ruby looked again at the color of her pet. A thought came to her and it made her smile. "I'll call you Red." The large red cockroach was a ruby red gem. *A gem no one sees the worth of, just like me.*

Trapped, Red was cozy and warm in her pocket. Ruby leaned up against a doorway, hoping a bit of warmth would wend its way between its cracks and over her skin. The roar of a train's whistle broke the silence. *Where are you tonight, Mother? Could you be looking out a window high above me wondering, "who is that little frozen girl beneath my balcony?" Or are you walking along the streets looking into the faces of children, trying to find me? Look into my face, Mother. I am here. Find me, please.* There was always a special fragrance about her mother. Lavender. *Dearest Mother, I am here waiting for you.*

Her teeth chattered together like ice cubes in the Mrs. Stone's water. She blew on her fingers. They felt as if they might just snap off one at a time. She examined her ashy skin and marveled at the sound of her own voice, for she had actually survived on the streets of New York City for one night and two days. Her hands, legs, and feet were so cold she could barely feel them any longer. As the city filled with snow, icicles hung two feet from the eaves of houses and trimmed the tree limbs like frosting.

Streetlights turned to snow globes, and snowdrifts crawled up spokes on wheels of carts and automobiles. Even the tall brick buildings seemed huddled together for warmth as the wind's tongue licked along the sides, searching for a small body to chill.

Steam from a close-by underground sewer swirled in the air. How she longed to sit on top of it so a bit of warmth would creep into her bones. Looking on all sides, she saw no one around. She slowly creeped to the manhole covering and plopped down. The steam flowed up beneath her filthy dress. The warmth was heavenly and rose on all sides of her. She felt like a dumpling steaming in a pot.

Her thoughts returned to the splendid house. Right about now, Miss Betsy would have her nightly ice cream with hot fudge sauce, her dolls beside her in bed. Mrs. Stone would be tucked in under heavy down quilts with a hot water bottle, surrounded by fancy plates of red meats and sweet chocolates. The Mrs. Stone often told Ruby she was in danger of "hell fire"—which didn't sound so bad right then, cold as she was. Tired, she slumped onto the hard, frozen earth. Ruby sank into a cold sleep.

"Hello? Are you sleeping? Are you hurt? Or are you dead?" A man touched her neck.

Ruby managed to open one eye. The man stood over her, dressed in all black like a funeral.

"I'm the sleeping dead. I've been expecting you." Ruby opened both eyes as he lifted her off the street. He looked like the man who had taken Papa Burke's body away after he crossed over.

"What's your name, dear one?" He walked with her in his arms.

"Ruby." She heard her voice shrinking like a balloon. Then, she remembered her jar and her pet. "Red."

"Well, Miss Ruby Red, I am taking you with me. Don't be afraid; I won't hurt you."

She didn't have enough strength to call out or to resist him. Where was he taking her? Was he an undertaker? Or was she in the arms of the angel of death crossing over to heaven? It didn't matter. The capacity to care had gone out of her. Shrunk from hunger on the inside and frozen on the outside. Maybe she'd crumble to pieces and blow away in the wind. Perhaps he was carrying her off to bury in his garden. Come spring, she'd love to have pretty flowers growing on the soil above her. Would Red hang around her grave, like a trusted dog pining for his dearly departed master? But first, he'd have to figure a way out of the jar. Ruby's thoughts faded into dreams.

6
...

"There you are." The voice came from the center of a bright light. Moments later, a face materialized in the glow. "Welcome, Ruby."

"Thank you for the heavenly reception." Ruby was overjoyed that her covetous actions with the porcelain doll and stealing the candy cane hadn't kept her out of Heaven. Now, she'd be with Papa Burke again. Maybe her mother had a home here, too. They could visit.

The heavenly being laughed. "This is not Heaven."

"But you're an angel—"

"I'm not an angel. I'm Miss Claire."

"But you look like just like an angel, ma'am. This place must have a gaggle of them. I think I've crossed over."

"Ruby, listen to me. You haven't crossed over, and this is not Heaven. When you were brought here, you were half frozen."

"Well, I'm thawed now." Ruby shook her head trying to get used to the fact she wasn't dead. It was then she became aware of lying on an old, saggy cot. Nope, this couldn't be Heaven.

The saintly woman sat on a small stool. The heavenly halo turned out to be pure winter light streaming through the window above the woman whose hair was blonde and skin was white as milk. She wore a long white dress with a lace collar. If there were such things as angels, Miss Claire would be in charge of them.

"You've been here two days, Ruby Red."

"But my name is Ruby—"

"Yes, I know, Ruby Red," Miss Claire interrupted. "The gentleman who brought you in told us. You were in such bad condition that the doctor said hypothermia might shut down your heart and breathing, so we wrapped you in heavy blankets and kept you by the fire. Many prayers were spoken, and here you are today, doing just fine." Miss Claire flung her hand over her heart. That's when Ruby decided it would not be polite to correct the person who just saved her life. At that moment in time, she became Ruby Red. It was an interesting feeling to wake up with a new name.

Propping herself up on an elbow, Ruby had a look at the room. It was a large space, empty of color but sure full of beds and chamber pots—enough to keep her busy a full day. Silently, she counted about 25 of each and was sure she was about to be told to empty them all. Carrying heavy baskets of clothes and emptying chamber pots seemed to be her lot in life. As long as she was warm and had food to eat, so be it.

Miss Claire smiled right into Ruby's face and kept on chattering. No white person had ever spoken to her for this long without telling her what needed to be cleaned. Ruby figured it'd be a show of good faith to start work without being asked, but when she pulled back the covers to get out of bed, she saw someone had changed her into a nightshirt. What had happened to her clothes? There, across the room on a wire hanger, hung her old dress now scrubbed clean.

"You're so thin. Stay right here in bed until you're stronger."

Ruby melted back into the covers. Somewhere, children laughed. The sound brought some peace of mind until she saw the bowl of liquid on a tray beside her bed. Not sure what it was, she hungered for something she could chew.

"Are you ready for some warm broth?" Miss Claire dipped the tip of the spoon into the soup and lifted it to her mouth.

"Smells like cabbage." She scrunched her face as she recalled shopkeeper's rotten green vegetables and the buggery Brussels sprouts. Her own words had come back to trouble her.

"At least try the cabbage broth. It has a piece or two of boiled chicken in it." Miss Claire coaxed, her voice waxing sweet.

Ruby peered down into the bowl. "Can't see chicken from here."

Miss Claire held the spoon to her mouth. "Where are your parents, Ruby? We need to notify them about your location."

"They're the ones who should be notifying *me* about *their* location." Ruby gathered all her politeness together and then some in order to open her mouth and accept the pale liquid into it. Ruby grimaced. It tasted spoiled.

"So you're an orphan."

"No, ma'am, not orphaned. My mother's lost. There's a difference."

"How long has your mother been lost?" She smiled halfway.

"About six years now." Ruby took the spoon and bowl into her own hands to feed herself. Miss Claire sat silently watching until Ruby had finished.

"I'll make sure it has more meat in it next time." Miss Claire set the empty bowl back on the tray. She took the bed covers between her long fingers and pulled them up to Ruby's neck. "Now just lie back and get more rest."

Not wanting to make a bad move, Ruby asked, "When can I get up?"

"Maybe tomorrow."

"Tomorrow'll be a good day; it always is." Ruby smiled up at her in the most pleasing manner she could muster. It was important that this woman continue to like her because Ruby sure liked Miss Claire.

The woman acted to be in a big hurry to leave the room, most likely the reason was to pile up a list of tomorrow's chores to be carried out now that Ruby was fully conscious again. Suddenly remembering Red, Ruby sat straight up. "Wait! Where's my jar? I had a small blue Mason jar. I have to have it!"

"Oh, you mean the jar with the food inside? Yes, it's right here." Miss Claire pulled it out from beneath the bed. Holding it up to the window she said, "The food looks rotten to me. I'll take it to the kitchen and have it washed out for you and then bring it right back." She turned again to leave.

"No!" Ruby cried, holding out her hand.

Shrugging, Miss Claire finally handed it to her. "You don't need to hoard food any longer. There's fresh food here for you to eat. Oh, and your little bit of kindling is under the bed, too. Just no lighting fires in the house, okay? Now get some rest, and I'll be back later to check on you."

Ruby watched her leave.

"Red! Red! Where are you?" Ruby gently shook the jar with a sinking feeling. Then, she saw the two little antennae as they began to slowly drum against the glass again. Miss Claire did not have a clue as to what was really inside of the container. Ruby smiled and settled back into her pillow, slipping the jar under the blankets.

7
...

By the next day, Ruby felt as though she had never been weak. Even Red seemed perkier. Finding a long string, she tied it tightly beneath the lid and about the lip of the jar, then hung it around her waist and slipped the jar into her pocket. In the other pocket, she hid the wood.

Ever since she started caring for Red, he had a good place to live, and now someone had given her a good place to live again. Things would be pretty perfect if only she could stop worrying about Papa Burke's ghost, wondering if he was aware she had disappeared from the grand house. Maybe, once the snow had gone and birds returned, she could sneak off to the cemetery for a day and explain where she had gotten off to, in case he needed to contact her. But for now, she needed to stay off the blizzardy streets. And if that was to happen, she better get to work and earn her keep.

Ruby waited days, and when no list of chores came, she swiftly gravitated to the kitchen to wash the big cook pots. She also chopped carrots and cut onions into chunks for boiling. It was a good place to be because she could slip a carrot end or a buttered roll into her mouth when no one was looking, and into her jar went a lump of sweet yam or a bit of fat for Red. It was more than any roach could possibly eat.

Myna was the main cook and boss of the food. With skin the color of milk chocolate, her eyes were of different sizes, spread far apart like the sun and the moon. She had a brisk smile and uneven teeth. She had twice the get-up-and-go of Mama Burke and was just as nice.

Mainly, there was silence between Myna and Ruby as they worked. It wasn't the strained silence of not knowing what to say, but the sweet, peaceful kind of silence between two friends who knew what needed to be done and went about doing it without the need for idle talk to fill the empty air. This gave way to questions that bumped into each other inside of Ruby's head until she could no longer resist.

"You sure have a lot of children in this place." Her dress sleeves were rolled up to her elbows as she washed heaps of silverware in soapy dishwater.

"They come from the same place as you, the streets. You seen how it's spilling over with children who got no home, no parents, nowhere to go! Mercy me! It's a dangerous place for young'uns and innocents like yourself. And if a lunatic don't slit your throat, then hunger'll kill you." Myna kept right on peeling potatoes.

"A lunatic?" It sounded like a word Ruby needed to know.

"Mean, crazy, mixed-up, ratty people." In the process of whirling her arms around in the air while she spoke, Myna dropped a potato. "No one wants to be around those people, no ma'am. You see a lunatic, you get away fast as you can."

"I met a lunatic. He hit me on the head." Ruby picked up the potato and handed it back to Myna.

"Well, here you're safe." Myna wrapped her arms around Ruby for a moment so she could feel the power of her words. "We feed and clothe all children from babies to teenagers. As you can see, we're overflowing with motherless children!" Myna let loose of Ruby before lifting a large pot of water onto the fire and dumping the potatoes into it.

"I'm not motherless. I have a mother. I just can't find her." This was an important distinction that no one but her seemed to understand. "When will the other mothers come for their children?"

"Mothers come for them? No, no, no. If they was coming, they'd be here by now. That goes for you, too." Myna's words stung Ruby, but Myna continued, "Meanwhile, our cup runneth over."

"What cup?"

"It means this place has more children than it can hold. We're busting at the seams like a fat woman in a girl's dress."

She opened the oven door wide and began to baste the plump turkey, dripping in its juices. Back in the mansion, a big turkey fed five people. Here, there were plenty more than five to feed.

"Will there be enough for everyone to have a bit of that, or is it just for the people who own this house?" Ruby's mouth watered.

"We all share alike! There's plenty for us all to have some meat. The good Lord provides. Do you say your prayers, girl? Now don't lie to me, you hear?"

"Never prayed before," Ruby answered, looking at her feet.

"What? Everyone needs prayers, specially the goodnight prayers to keep you safe while you're asleep. God looks after us when we can't look after ourselves."

"Don't know how." Ruby felt her cheeks flush and her neck warm.

"You got a voice, right? Just open up your mouth and talk like you're talking to me right now, but instead you be talking to Him." Myna pointed out the window toward the sky. "God is great, and He guides us. Remember that, child, when you feeling low."

It seemed to Ruby that Myna's mouth also runneth over with useful information. Ruby cocked her head to the side. "Do you tell all the children about God and prayers?"

"Just the ones who work in the kitchen." Myna winked.

"How many has that been?"

"You're the first," Myna laughed, now pulling bread from the oven. The smell of the yeast made Ruby wild with hunger. "Pretty soon, all these children will be leaving, and new ones will take their place."

"Leave here? Where are they going?"

"To good homes, I hope. A train takes them out west, clear into Texas. I hear tell it's really something to see people stand along the way and flag it down just so they can have a New York child. If they see one they want, they take them right home with them then and there. The children are given beds to sleep in, food to eat, and a safe place to live. Another trainload leaves late spring."

"Oh Myna, I want to go on that train."

"Naw, you can't go. The train's just for white children. You'll stay here in the city. It's just how things are."

"Only white children find a home? Doesn't seem fair." Ruby shook her head.

"Not all things that look fair, are fair." Myna winked at her. "Just how the world works."

"I don't understand."

"Some of the children on the train leave here with sisters and brothers. But most times, they get split up. One child goes to one family while another one goes to another family, sometimes miles away. Some families only want one child." Myna shook her head.

"That's awful!"

"It is awful." Myna spoke softly. "I don't go with them on the train because I can't stand to see it happen. Some families do take in more, though, keeping siblings together."

"They've already lost so much. And then to lose even more." Ruby's chin quivered.

"Sometimes, families want a hooligan in their family to help with chores around the farm. But the surprise turns out to be on the family when the hooligan runs off or is mean to the people who took him in."

"Are hooligans like lunatics?"

"More like first cousins. You see, just before the train leaves, Miss Anna and Miss Claire go to the jailhouse and get all these street kids released into their custody, and then they load them onto the train. It's their last chance for a better life. The Orphan Train drops them with a new family, in the middle of wheat fields and cornfields."

Myna held out her arm and pointed as if she could see it from where she stood.

Ruby shivered at the word "orphan," but living in a field of food seemed like the perfect life. She'd eat until her tummy grew nice and round, and then she'd lie down to sleep in a clean bed, right after being tucked in on all sides by those goodnight prayers.

"This time, the last stop is in Texas, in a town called Denton." Myna scrubbed the counter.

Lost in daydreams, Ruby began to heat oil for frying the cut potatoes when Miss Claire walked into the kitchen bringing news.

8
...

"Ruby, great news! I found a home for you right here in the city!" Miss Claire proudly announced.

"Praise the Lord!" Myna said, clapping her hands together and smiling one of her beautiful smiles.

"You found my mother! I knew it would happen."

Miss Claire continued talking, "No, I already told you that it would be impossible to find your mother, especially after so long."

"Oh. Well, I don't think I want to stay here in the city anymore anyway. Not when there are far off fields of food waiting."

Myna snorted.

"What are you talking about?"

"Miss Myna told me about the Orphan Train. Please put me on it."

"It's not possible, Ruby." Miss Claire was gentle with her words.

"I already explained it to her," Myna said quickly.

"But I do have something for you, Ruby. A fine elderly lady by the name of Mrs. Perkins had to let her maid go, and she wants someone young and strong to take her place.

I thought of you. It's perfect. She even has a room for you just off the kitchen. I saw it. It's sunny and has—"

"I can't stay *here*?" Ruby's voice quivered over the unexpected send-off.

"No, you cannot stay here," Miss Claire explained.

Ruby's face showed the shock she felt. She stumbled to say something, but her words quit on her.

"And why can't she stay here in the kitchen with me?" Myna took up for Ruby. She turned from the heated stove with a ball of anger welled up in her eyes. Her hands were on her hips, and she shook her head. "So you've found her a place to stay where she can work her fingers to the bone, huh? Lord, help us! When will things change for us?"

Ruby had never heard a black woman backtalk a white woman before. She feared the police would be called in lickety-split. She took a giant step backwards, not wanting to get run over by them coming through the door to carry Myna away.

"It's the best I can do under the circumstances, Myna. We have so many children to place. It is much better than being out on the street." Miss Claire remained devoutly calm.

"Then put me on the train with the other children!" Ruby pleaded, feeling a sudden boldness come over her.

"No, I can't. The train is only for white children. There are nearly a hundred here at the orphanage, and there's only room for about four dozen on the train as it is. You have no idea what a rare opportunity this job is for you, Ruby. Mrs. Perkins will buy you two dresses and one pair of shoes a year. You will have a room all to yourself. You'll never go hungry again, and most of all, you'll be safe and off the streets."

It was obvious Miss Claire had no inkling what a household could be like with a nasty old crow running the place, but Myna did. Ruby weighed it in her heart. If she stayed in the city, she would still be close to Mama Burke and Papa Burke's ghost—though he had yet to pay her a visit—and to Myna. Even if she never saw any of them ever again, she would be happy to know she was near them. The same sky was above them all, and if she looked up at it, then she'd feel they all were together in the same round bowl with memories connecting to them all like stars.

Grease bubbled, popped, and spit in the large fry pan. Myna wasn't ready to dump her cut-up potatoes into the grease just yet. To ensure the pan didn't catch fire, Ruby quickly picked up the handle of the pan to move it off the stove. The greasy handle slipped from her hands, spilling the hot oil down the front of her. The oil ran down her legs and pooled about her feet. Being fried alive, Ruby screamed, feeling she stood in hell's water. Miss Claire and Myna quickly worked together to remove all her clothes and set her in a large tub, dumping cool water into it. Myna ran to the icebox for ice. In her haste, ice slipped from her hands and slid every which way across the floor.

"Stop!" Miss Anna shouted. "Water only makes it worse. Help me lift her out of the tub."

With great care, the women picked Ruby up and set her on her feet. Ruby took a step and then slipped on the ice, causing her to fall hard on her right knee. She felt something pop and her kneecap swam to the right of her leg.

Miss Anna went for the doctor.

"Lord, help this girl!" Myna hollered her prayer as they helped Ruby to bed.

Ruby writhed back and forth in pain until tears poured over her mouth and nose like water off a roof in rainstorm. Ruby's screams drew the attention of the children. They pressed together in the doorway to see what happened. No matter how often they were shooed away, they always came back.

Within an hour, Doctor Weber walked calmly through the door. "Sorry I couldn't come right away. I still had patients in the waiting room." He set his leather medical bag on a chair and unwound the scarf from his neck.

"At least you're here now. Follow us, Doctor."

The women led the doctor up the back steps to the room where Ruby lay on a cot, wrapped in a blanket. The pain was a double-edged sword so intense it caused Ruby to lose consciousness but also so powerful that it kept bringing her back. A fever raged, and incoherently, she rambled on about Red and her mother.

Doctor Weber pulled back the blankets covering the girl. When he saw Ruby's legs, his face twisted up in horror. Then he mouthed to the women who stood over him that he wasn't sure he could do much. "Not only is she burned, but she also tore her patellar tendon just below the knee. Only surgery can fix it. I'll do what I can do make it manageable."

Myna bit her lip.

"What I can do is tend to her burns. I need bowls of clean water and tear sheets for bandages. The burned skin has to be scrubbed off. I'll need all of your help to hold her down. Hold her tightly. One of you take hold of her ankles and the other two, an arm each. Okay, girl, bite down on this kitchen sponge because this is going to hurt. I'm sorry."

Ruby couldn't process what was said, but she did know when they took hold of her and began scrubbing. She kept twisting and turning, trying to get away from everyone touching her. Being electrocuted by a lightning bolt couldn't hurt more than this. Ruby hollered so loud that her nose began to bleed. She screamed until she had no more voice.

Beads of sweat poured down the doctor's brow as he worked. Finally, he looked up at the women. "If she keeps contracting her legs from the pain, her new skin won't stretch, and she won't have full use of that limb which will result in a bad limp."

"Can't you give her anything for the pain?" Miss Claire hollered.

"Well, I could give her a shot of morphine, but it's expensive."

"I'll pay for it," Miss Anna answered quietly, her voice ripe with pity.

Doctor Weber drew a glass bottle and long needle from his black leather bag. Holding it up to the light of the window, he watched through his round glasses until there was enough liquid in the shot. When a tiny bit of the liquid spouted out, Dr. Weber headed toward Ruby with it and stuck it quickly into her arm. "Give it a minute to work." He wiped her feverish head with a cool cloth.

True to his word, the drug worked, making Ruby groggy. Only aware the doctor was now making adjustments to her other leg and knee, she couldn't feel it. Right then, he could have cut the whole thing off, and she wouldn't have budged an inch. Hours later, she awoke to both legs straightened and rolled in cloth. It made moving around nearly impossible. The pain soon returned like a volcano. Ruby spent endless nights chewing on her bed sheets to keep from screaming from the intolerable pain. Liquid oozed from between the bandages. The leg with the torn tendon was the worst. She kept tugging at the bandages, loosening them so she could bend that leg. She had been instructed not to do so, but in the face of pain, a little relief was her only friend.

Lying in bed for weeks without company, Ruby spent time holding up the jar to her face so she could talk to Red. She felt isolated, and thoughts of her mother frenzied her. "Maybe my mother will find work here at the orphanage, and Miss Ida will ask her to carry some cabbage soup with invisible pieces of chicken upstairs to the girl with the fried legs. When she walks into this room, she'll see me here in this bed. 'There you are! What have you done to yourself, girl? I'm here now, and I will take care of you forever,' she'll say to me. Then I'll say to her, 'I knew you would come for me.' She'll sit down on this bed next to me and sing in a voice that will calm my soul until all the pain I feel will vanish into a little speck of dust to blow out that window." Daily, Ruby's eyes searched the doorway for her mother in the red coat, but she never came.

Every few days, the bandages were changed, each time revealing legs shrunken from lack of use. The skin continued to crack and bleed. Although ointment was applied for scaring and to aid in the healing process, the accident left Ruby's legs disfigured.

"Maybe with time you'll be able to use that leg and knee again. Staying in bed for so long may have made matters worse. Come on, time you get yourself up and moving." Miss Anna helped her up.

Miss Claire and Miss Anna got on either side of Ruby and lifted her out of her bed, helping her to her feet. Ruby tried to figure out how to make her legs work again so she could walk. The women helped her move across the room where they stopped in front of a full-length mirror. Ruby could plainly see that her left leg dangled off the ground an inch above the other. When she put both feet on the floor, the rest of her looked lopsided.

"Being in bed for all these weeks didn't do me any favors. I look bent."

Miss Ida sighed.

"It's not that big of a deal, Ruby," Miss Anna told her.

Ruby lowered her eyes to her chest. It was a big deal to her. "My parts are wearing out, and I ain't even old yet."

9

New York, Springtime 1921

It was the first warm day of spring. Ruby was given a cane and helped outside to enjoy the day. By her choice, she sat alone as a flock of screaming children frantically played nearby in the fresh air, crazed over the change of season.

Ruby watched the pair of blonde twins. Emily and Amy always sat next to one another at the dinner table, and now, outside, they held one another's hands as though they might be separated at any moment. The only way to tell them apart was by Emily's shorter hair. Ruby would talk to them if they strode her way. They seemed content with one another, though—no need for anyone else.

While experienced in dealing with adults, Ruby had no practice with other children. She wasn't sure how to interact with them or how to get them to like her. It reminded her of a story Papa Burke had told her once about a dog. The dog was so used to playing with cats that when another dog came along, it died of fright. She decided that being alone was better, especially since her accident.

Thanks to Miss Anna, she now had a cane to help her walk. The tip was good for drawing pictures in the soft spring earth.

"What's that supposed to be?" a small voice asked quizzically.

That's when she saw him for the first time. His hair was the color of flames, and he had playful eyes like city skies expecting rain—blue with shadows of gray. As Ruby spoke, a light came over him as if a glorious story were about to touch his ears.

"This is me, and this is my mother."

"She's very pretty."

She scribbled lines through her private picture.

"Everyone said I was too scared to talk to you. But I'm not. See? I'm right here, talking away, and I want to know what happened to your legs."

Ruby sized up the narrow-shouldered ruffian and thought him to be about the same age she had been when Papa and Mama Burke found her on the street. A smile slid up the side of her face, thinking how to send him away, sufficiently frightened, to the other side of the yard. "Fried 'em to a crisp!"

Andy adamantly shook his head. "I heard you were born that way."

"Well, you heard wrong. I wasn't born this way, and those who have been here for a few months know all about it. They just aren't telling you the truth." Ruby looked at the heap of kids looking their way in curiosity. "I can see that you're brave. I'll tell you the truth, but *only* if you're sure you can stomach it." Ruby narrowed her eyes at him.

"Yup." Fully curious, he leaned in. "I got a good stomach."

"That's a good thing, too, because you're going to need it

when you hear about my legs. A while ago, the kids here learned not to mess with me."

"Why not?" Andy asked, perplexed.

"I got a bad temper. And if someone messes with me, I'm apt to do something violent. The last time, I got out the frying pan, poured oil in, heated it up, and fried up my own legs." She crossed her eyes.

"Why'd you do that?" The boy flinched.

"Felt like it." Ruby snapped a finger.

"What'd you get so mad about?"

"Stuff. I also tore up my knee. Makes me limp at times."

"Maybe you should've fried up the other kid's legs instead of yours."

"No, that's not polite."

He looked over his shoulder at children staring at them from afar and then back at Ruby. "Does it hurt?"

"Maybe it'd hurt someone else, someone like *you* or someone like *them*, but not *me*."

His voice got whispery. "Everyone is afraid of you and won't come near."

"Good." She conjured up some wickedness she felt deep down inside. Closing one eye, she flailed her arms in the air. "See, I'm a lunatic!"

The other children screamed and ran further away.

"I'm Andy."

"I'm Ruby Red."

"Keen name. Let me have a look at your legs? Do they look fried?" he said, touching her bandages with his dirty fingers.

"No, you can't see them." Ruby hastily pulled back,

thinking about the skin that looked like red pox filled with crispy blisters. "No one can."

"Is that why you have them wrapped up like a cocoon?"

"None of your business!" Ruby pushed him out of the way with her cane, but Andy didn't waiver. He seemed to be single minded and independent. She liked those qualities. "I do have something special to show you, if you want to see it."

"I want to see it! What is it?" Andy leaped up and down.

Ruby pulled the bottle from her pocket and showed him Red who leaned up against the side of the jar, waving his antennae in greeting.

"Swell!"

Just then, Miss Anna stood by the door and called to Ruby. "Come on inside. It's time to change those bandages."

Ruby slipped the jar back into her pocket and used the cane to struggle to her feet.

"Can we be friends?" Andy scrunched his eyes against the sun.

"Maybe. I'll consider it in my goodnight prayers when and if I decide to say them. And Andy? I didn't really fry them up. I had an accident in the kitchen. I don't want you to be scared of me."

"Don't worry, Ruby. Someday, those legs will get unwrapped and turn into something beautiful like—" just then, a monarch sailed past on delicate wings "—like a butterfly!" Andy held out his arms as if he were flying and ran off.

10
.....

Spring continued to flood the city with its rain.

The hills of snow had melted, absorbing into the soil and sky, pulling forth warm earth with air. The excitement at the orphanage crescendoed into high-pitch passion as the time for the children to travel west grew closer.

The same day Ruby was to meet Mrs. Perkins, dozens of children were preparing for their journey west. Jittery, Ruby helped Myna pack food for their trip. It had been a long time since she was allowed in the kitchen. Ruby tip toed into the room and looked around. There was no evidence in the room that anything bad had ever taken place. Her legs wore the only evidence. They still cracked and bled. She was able to bend her right knee a little now, but one leg would always remain a bit shorter than the other. Outside of a miracle, there was no cure.

Dozens of crates were filled with food for the journey. Myna and Ruby dumped oranges, apples and grapes into them. Others held buckets of butter and loaves of bread. Others overflowed with slabs of cured sliced meat, boiled eggs, and jugs of fresh water for drinking. Closing her eyes, Ruby tried to imagine a world beyond this place and longed to be one of the travelers on that westward train.

"Lots of children are riding on this train today. Some older boys'll be released from the jailhouse today that's going, too. Maybe country air and hard work will get their attitudes right. I'm afraid Miss Claire and Miss Anna are gonna have they hands full with the likes of them hooligans, along with all the babies and the little children packed inside of those cars." Myna shook her head with worry. "It's a long trip. I thank God we'll be getting extra help from the convent so I won't be managing alone with the children staying here. I went once with the train and decided that was enough for me. Too much sadness. Better I stay put. Besides, what I know, I know about here. Too many different ways of doing things out there. I'm too old to learn the new."

"You ain't old, Myna."

"If I ain't old, then what?" Myna hid a beautiful smile behind her hand.

"Perfect. You're perfect."

Myna's eyes filled with what looked like love. After a pause, she said, "Here, I have something for you. Just saving it for this day." She took a dress down off a hook on the back of the kitchen door. Myna held it up for Ruby to see how bright and blue it was before helping her into it. Putting a big red bow at the back of Ruby's hair, Myna smiled. "We always send our children off with new clothes. I know this dress is a bit long, but it'll cover your legs. Keep it pulled way down to your ankles. You'll be fine." Myna stepped back to look at Ruby up and down.

"Thank you. I'm glad it ain't drab."

Myna slapped her hand over her heart. "You look

wonderful. God be with you, child!"

Ruby could tell by the power of Myna's words how she felt about her. What gift did she have to give? "Myna, I want you to know that I said a goodnight prayer for God to take care of you." It was the best she could do on such short notice.

"Prayers are just as powerful during the daylight. Come on, walk with me while I carry these boxes to the wagons."

"I can help." Ruby went for a large box, but Myna stepped in and handed her a small sack to carry instead. With the sack in one hand, she leaned on the cane in the other.

Ruby slowly followed Myna through the kitchen door and into the yard. They walked around the side of the building and followed the path out to the street where wagons waited to take the children to the train station. There was someone she had developed a fondness for, and she had to say goodbye to him. Andy was so little and cute; someone was sure to pick him first. There he was, standing second in line, looking all pouty faced and frightened.

Ruby passed the sack to Myna and went to Andy.

Andy glanced sideways. "I get to ride a train today, Ruby. I ain't so sure that's a good thing."

"It's a good thing, Andy. You mustn't worry."

"I don't know about trains. They're really loud." Andy quivered.

"But they look like so much fun to ride!" Ruby imagined.

"Are you and Red coming, too?" His voice was pleading.

"No, there's work to do in the city." Ruby willed herself to keep a strong heart.

"Then I'll stay, too." Andy's voice shook with emotion

as he stepped out of the line.

"Andy, you can't." A train whistle blew from the station two miles away. "Listen to the sound of that whistle, Andy."

"It's loud. It hurts my ears." His chin sunk into his shoulders.

"Time to leave! Follow me in a straight line please! I said to get into a straight line!" Miss Claire ordered.

"Say goodbye to Red for me," Andy hollered as he climbed up into a wagon.

"I will." Ruby slipped her hand into her pocket and felt the glass jar.

A fight started between some of the older boys who had just been released from the jailhouse. "Young men! Put those clods of dirt down, or I shall march you right back to where you have been staying, and there you shall remain until you are grown men!" Miss Claire waved a switch in the air.

Ruby was turning back when she saw the twins, Emily and Amy, holding one another's hands. "Goodbye, Emily. Goodbye, Amy," she whispered. "Be safe. Be happy."

11

Then, it was time for Ruby's new journey.

"Come on, girl. We took care of those traveling kids. Now it's, time for you to go to your new home." Myna squeezed her hand. Ruby kept stealing backward glances until the street took a turn. The sounds of horses' shoed hooves striking the bricked streets as they pulled the wagons filled with children along lingered for several minutes, but that, too, faded at last. Myna walked slowly, but Ruby struggled to keep up with Myna's pace. They passed tall brownstone homes on tree-lined avenues. Big black oak trees budded out; in another month, pedestrians would enjoy their canopy of shade. The last time she was in this part of town, the snow was nearly impossible to walk through. She was sure Mrs. Stone's house was close.

In no time at all, Myna and Ruby stood in front of Ruby's new home, but it was like *deja-vous*. Three stories high and all Ruby could think about was all those stairs. Myna excitedly pushed the doorbell, wanting to hear its chimes as Ruby climbed the steps, one at a time. A butler opened the door. He didn't look anything like Papa Burke. This one was skinny and didn't smile. He also spoke with a funny accent and left them standing in the large circular hallway while he went to call the lady of the house. Oriental rugs graced the shiny marble floor beneath their feet. A hanging crystal chandelier reminded Ruby of icicles hanging from rooftops in the winter. Prisms of rainbow colors shot through the room and onto the painted walls.

"Oh, Ruby!" Myna gasped with elation. "You'll be living in such a fine house among hundreds of beauteous things to look at."

"Every one in need of dusting."

"Behave. The Lord's got a plan for everything." Myna grabbed Ruby's walking stick and quickly set it in a corner. "No sense drawing attention."

Tottery Mrs. Perkins entered the hallway wearing a long, shiny black dress that had bits of lace at her neckline and at the ends of her sleeves. Her gray hair was drawn up into a bun at the back of her head. In one hand, she held an organdy hankie and in the other, a mahogany cane. Ruby swallowed giggles as she thought about them tapping their way together through the big house. The woman's clear blue eyes looked Ruby over as if making her mind up about something. Once she silently arrived at her decision, she greeted Ruby warmly.

"How nice to meet you, Ruby Red," Mrs. Perkins beamed with a curt nod of the head.

"Nice to meet you, too, ma'am," Ruby replied, keeping her eyes on her shoes like Papa Burke taught her. She felt herself becoming wobbly due to her stiffness from standing for too long in one spot. If she took a step without her cane right now, she'd topple over. Her fingertips were prickly with nerves.

"What a polite young girl you have here," Mrs. Perkins said to Myna, clearly pleased.

"Yes, ma'am." Myna kept her eyes lowered, too.

"Come and sit by me, dear," she said, showing Ruby into the living room.

Taking a hold of Myna's arm, Ruby jiggled her leg to release her locked knee and then laboriously limped along.

"Why are you limping, dear?" Mrs. Perkins's pleased voice shifted to one of alarm.

"It was just a little mishap, ma'am. I can still work very hard."

"Is that so? I wonder if you will be able to manage these stairs and carry loads?" she asked.

"Would all the loads be heavy ones?" Ruby gulped.

Mrs. Perkins pulled Ryby's long skirt up above her knees to see both legs heavily bandaged. A look of sheer revulsion seized the old woman's face. "Oh, my goodness gracious! What on earth happened to you?"

There was no revelation from the heavens, but quite suddenly, Ruby knew she didn't want to live here after all, which made her get an idea worthy of any lunatic. Crossing her eyes, she turned her head in such a way that Myna couldn't see. "I fried 'em up in hot oil during one of my fits, ma'am." She looked up at the woman with a wide smile and a cross-eyed gaze.

"Ruby!" Myna gasped as she took her by the shoulders and tried shaking some sense into her.

Mrs. Perkins staggered backwards and grabbed onto the brooch she wore high on the neck of her dress as though it had special powers to keep her standing upright.

Ruby wondered if the lady was about to be sick. She hoped Mrs. Perkins would turn her head to the side so it wouldn't be on the new blue dress that Myna had just given to her.

"Ruby!" Myna scolded. "What would make you say something like that? Mrs. Perkins, what happened to Ruby's legs was an accident. She's still healing but should be fine. I apologize for the outburst. You must forgive Ruby. She's just frightened."

Vehemently, the elderly lady shook her head. "I must withdraw my offer to hire her, for I simply cannot have a disfigured servant who is unable to work hard," the woman said flatly. "And one with a bad temper as well."

"Ruby?" Myna looked angry.

Wanting to show Myna she at least tried, she answered, "Excuse me, ma'am, but I can work hard. I'll show you." Ruby glanced around for something heavy to lift. With an idea still rolling about inside her head, she reached for the tall glass oil lamp with a hand painted globe. Grabbing it, she then allowed it to slip from her hands. It crashed onto the floor and broke into a hundred pieces.

"Oh dear, let's clean that up." Franticly, Myna looked for the kitchen to get a broom.

"No." A forked blue vein on Mrs. Perkins's forehead appeared as she spoke, making her eyelids twitch. "Just leave before she decides it's *my* legs that need frying next."

The butler quickly escorted Myna and Ruby to the door, as the woman observed. Ruby decided one could never go wrong for being polite, even if it was not called for. "Thank you, ma'am. Have a nice day now." She uncrossed her eyes, snatched up her walking stick, and walked out the front of the house.

Outside again, in the springtime air, Ruby heard Red rattling on the inside of the jar. *I am feeling better now, Red. Can you tell it? Is my heart beating slower?*

"What made you say and do such things? You have your ways—hard-headed ways. I guess it's just as well. You would have just worked yourself into an early grave taking care of her splendid house." Myna's nose was pointed up in the air. Her jaw set. "Tell me something, Ruby: did you drop that lamp on purpose?"

"I don't believe I understand the question, Myna." Ruby pursed her lips and decided to not answer any more unnecessary questions today. She'd just enjoy the walk ahead of them.

Right then, the train whistle blew in short spurts. "The train will pull out of the station any minute now." One of Myna's beautiful smiles spread across her face. By the time the whistle blasted again, Myna pulled Ruby by the arm and hollered, "Hurry, girl!"

Ruby's legs and knees were rigid causing her to lose her footing here and there. She kept dropping her cane.

"Myna, you're hurting me. I can't go so fast."

Myna continued pulling her along without answering—never stopping.

"Don't go so quick. I can't keep up!" Ruby stumbled and grabbed onto a tree to keep upright. "Wait! I need my cane."

"Never mind that. We got just enough time. Now hurry!"

Ruby tried to stop to rub her achy, burning legs. But Myna grabbed hold of her arm harder than ever, and drug her to the station where they rushed onto the wooden platform, now empty of children. The Great Western locomotive began inching down the tracks like a hound sniffing out the Promised Land.

Excitement shot through Ruby like electricity then. It took her only an instant to realize she was feeling hope and that she wanted to experience it for the rest of her life. In that instant, Ruby made up her mind that she was going, too. Now was her chance. If she didn't take it, she would regret it forever. Ruby jerked from Myna and then took five steps toward the moving train. She watched for the step openings that would allow her entry to the boxcars. Reaching out, she tried to grab hold of one of the railings to hoist herself up on the steps. But the train was moving too fast for her, and she stumbled and fell, skidding along the wooden platform. Myna shouted out her name. Undeterred, Ruby quickly got to her feet and tried again with the same disappointing results. Suddenly, arms went about her waist. Her legs left the ground, and she was swept up on the train's steps just before the train picked up more speed. Looking back, she saw it had been the station master who helped her.

"What do I do now? Where am I going, Myna?" Ruby yelled as she latched onto the handle at the top of the metal steps, saying her daylight prayers not to tumble off.

"Home! You're going home, Ruby!" Myna framed her hands around her mouth to be heard above the roar of the engines.

"Where is home?"

"You'll know when you get there!"

"But how will I know?" Ruby felt the rumble of the train picking up speed. She felt exhilarated and frightened at the same time.

"Your heart will tell you. God's got you in the palm of His hand. Everything will turn out alright!"

Ruby watched Myna wave goodbye to her, knowing full well she would never again see Myna's face again in this lifetime. To keep from crying, she focused on the fleshy, loose part of Myna's arm that was waving like a flag caught in a thunderstorm. The movement of the train on the tracks felt like the earth was parting ways with itself. Heavy black smoke from the engines and the screech of steel wheels permeated the air. Ruby's adventure had launched.

12

The train had more children than seats, which meant Ruby stood.

To keep from falling, she gripped the back of seats. The erratic movements jostled her about, and at times she lost her balance. It was like being a marble tucked inside a tin can shaken by someone with a bad temper. She was getting a taste of Red's life. Eventually finding a place, Ruby sat on the wood plank floor.

Her legs throbbed. She felt weak. Biting her lip, she blinked hard to keep back the tears she so wanted to cry. Her good knee was badly bruised from all the tumbles she took while being pulled through the streets of New York. Lifting the string on the jar, she checked on Red. He was managing quite well and holding on to a piece of breakfast toast. "Good boy, Red."

Miss Claire and Miss Anna were caring for children from babies to teenagers, just as Myna had said. Needing to go unnoticed, Ruby turned her back to them, fearing they might stop the train to set her outside to walk back.

If her mother was not up in heaven, perhaps she was at one of the train stops. Or maybe somewhere on the tracks. Her mother would see her and say, "There you are! I lost you in the crowd. I have been looking for you ever since.

You have grown so tall and so beautiful, but I would still know my little girl anywhere."

Ruby turned around only to face Miss Claire who stooped to look her in the face.

"What are you doing on the train? You're supposed to be working for Mrs. Perkins," she said with a tough voice, but kindness still showed in her angel eyes.

Ruby shrugged her shoulders as if she had turned left instead of right and mysteriously ended up here. Miss Claire waited for her answer. She straightened her back and tapped the toe of her shoe. Finally, Ruby blurted, "She said I was disfigured!"

"I'm so sorry." Miss Claire pulled Ruby to her feet and held her tightly.

"Maybe you can find me a family, too!" Ruby sobbed into her shoulder.

"I don't think that's possible."

"Cause I'm ugly? You can tell me if I am. I saw my face in a mirror." Ruby jerked away.

"Ruby, stop talking like that. You cannot keep thinking of yourself as ugly. You are very pretty. But you're at the age in your life when you need to be practical." Miss Claire looked around at the little ones who had become frightened with their new surroundings. "Maybe it's good you've come. You can help Miss Anna and me. Then you can return with us back to New York. The last stop is Denton, Texas, our turning-around point. Think of this as a trip of a lifetime for you to always remember. You can stay back at the orphanage until another house opens to you. Don't worry now, dear."

"No, I ain't going back!"

Miss Claire tried to calm Ruby when a scuffle broke out between two older boys.

Ruby stared at the boys pushing and slugging one other. As one fell out of his seat and landed on the floor, two others jumped on top of him. Heaviness flowed through every inch of Ruby as she realized one of them was the teenage boy who had whacked her with the piece of wood and stolen her food: Louie.

He looked up at her and smiled a toothy grin. She starred straight into his face and scowled. He stuck his tongue out at her. She returned it.

"Louie!" Miss Claire scolded him. "You stop your shenanigans right this minute. Sit down and behave yourself. Do you understand?"

Louie nodded his head and then slumped back into the seat, all the while laughing to show the other boys he was tough. Flexing his muscles, he let everyone know he was the leader.

"Miss Claire, why do the older, mean boys get a home, and I don't?"

Miss Claire took a deep breath. "These boys will most likely end up working on farms."

No way could she work on a farm, not in her crippled condition.

"Let me try to find a seat for you." Miss Claire began looking for a spot.

"She can sit here with me, Miss Claire!" a small voice called from the back of the car.

"Okay, thank you." Miss Claire responded.

"Howdy, Ruby! You did come! You did come!" The voice belonged to a small red-headed boy who catapulted himself between his seat and the ceiling.

"Andy!" Ruby had never been so happy to see anyone.

"Sit on this seat with me. I thought I'd never see you again, but here you are!" Still bouncing up and down, he waved his arms above his head.

Ruby nodded and carefully held on to the back of the seats as she slowly walked to where Andy bounced. He shared the seat with two other small children who were crying because of his jumping.

"I'm littler, so I'll sit on your lap," Andy said.

Ruby smoothed the back of her dress with her hands and sat down. Perched on Ruby's lap gave Andy a suitable view out the window. She constantly reminded him not to kick her legs with his small feet as he moved about and helped calm the frightened children.

"Where's your cane?" he asked looking around.

"Back in New York somewhere." Ruby leaned her head on the back of the seat.

"Do you still have Red?"

"Of course." Ruby pulled out the jar and handed it to Andy.

"I think it must get stuffy in there. He needs some fresh air. Don't you think he would be happier living in the trees and grass?"

"What're you talking about? This jar is Red's home. Here, Red has food to eat, and he's safe from harm." Ruby realized her words were the same words Miss Claire used about Mrs. Perkins's employment.

"But just look, Ruby, it's a jar, just a glass jar. Don't keep him trapped. Set him free."

"I'm not so sure. You see, Red and me, we've been through a lot together during our short lives. People don't like cockroaches, and they don't like me either. Red and I, well, we belong together."

Andy put his feet on the cushion and moved Ruby's hair out of the way so he could whisper into her ear. "You have me now; you can let Red go free. He might meet a wife and have a bug sack of babies."

"We'll see." Andy had given her a lot to think about. His words tugged at her heart. She loved Red, but she knew she was keeping him trapped. It was wrong of her to make him live inside the jar forever. Maybe it was time to do what was best for him. Freedom was always preferable.

13

"Look at that!"

Ruby gasped as she looked out the train window. Factories melted into houses, which in turn, gave way to farms and fields, finally opening to a grand expanse of land where an eagle soared in circles over the tops of tall trees. But the lift of the hills was the finest sight.

"Look, no buildings! I see trees and lots of them! Look, Red!" Andy held the jar up so the roach could look out the window. "What do you think of that, Red? Hey, he didn't answer me, Ruby. I think a cat got his tongue!"

Ruby's eyes became wild with both excitement and fear all at once. Never in her dreams had she imagined so much land without bricks, stone, or pavement. And sky! There was so much sky that she felt overcome by it. Would she step outside and float away into it? Up until today, she had only seen a thin slice of smoky sky wedged between city buildings. This was a better plan. It was nature's original plan that people fouled up when they built cities to hold themselves prisoner. The sky was enormous. She put her hand on the windowpane and spread her fingers wide, needing to see the land frame by frame; it was overwhelming any other way. In between, she saw endless fields of flowers. Her mind was made up. Yes, this is where Red belonged. She loved him enough to finally let him go.

"How d'you suppose those trees and flowers got planted clear out here, Andy?"

"Don't know." He shook his head, wondering the same.

"Maybe God rained them down to cheer tired-out travelers."

"I wish I could roll around in it." Andy tried to figure out how to leap from the train. "If there are hills out there, I'm going to roll down them, too! I just hope there aren't any bears in them. They would eat me up with their big sharp teeth. Arg!" He lunged forward curving his fingers like claws.

"I'll protect you from bears. No one and nothing will hurt you while I'm around." Ruby put her arm around him.

"Thanks, Ruby." He settled back into her arms. Some of his wildfire hairs poked into her nose, making it itch.

Banks of flowers grew from the land, infusing the air with a light scent in the warm afternoon sunlight. The shiny steel train sliced the land in two pieces as the children filled the boxcars with loud talk and disorderly laughter. Ruby thought to herself that this place she was going to might just be Heaven. There was still time to figure out a way to stay there.

Andy hugged Ruby, and Ruby hugged Andy right back. They were heading to a place they had never been, explorers together. Soon, Red would forge his own way through tall blades of grass, around stones, and maybe up a tree to the very top where he could see the entire countryside—quite a feat for a common city roach. There was a silent communion between the three of them: Red, Ruby, and Andy. They shared a singleness of courage and a kind of insight that rarely exists.

By nightfall, a full white moon loomed in the sky, spattering its light across the steel engine. Stars floated above, and prairie flowers sank into the shadows, disappearing from the reflections of the train windows, which carried now sleeping children west. But Ruby didn't dare sleep yet. She would take all these images and memories with her through life. Right then and there, Ruby decided when she became a woman, she would return to walk through these fields that had no buildings to clutter the view.

During the night, a few children became sick from the fumes of the engine fuel. Ruby felt headachy and nauseated herself. At last, her eyes grew heavy, and her weary head slipped down until her chin almost rested on her chest.

14

By daylight, Ruby moved about her seat in discomfort. She needed to use a toilet, but there was none on the train. All the children cried loudly with the same ailment, and the teenage boys threatened to pee out the windows, which made everyone scream.

"Our first stop is this morning. But first, we'll make a short stop at the outskirts of town to wash up in a stream and change into new clothes." Miss Anna handed out boiled eggs.

Ruby arched her brows in thought. Her mother might be fishing in that stream! She had to be somewhere—why not there? And she'd say, "Do you like fish, Ruby girl? Come sit beside me. We will celebrate finding each other with a big fish dinner."

"Stop daydreaming, Ruby." Miss Anna nudged her. "Help peel eggs for the younger children."

Ruby did so, and when she had finished, she noticed Louie with his cap pulled down just far enough on his forehead that his eyes couldn't be seen, yet he could still see everyone and everything. Ruby felt a pang of pure hate. She wanted to imagine all sorts of torturous things happening to him, but she wouldn't give into her thoughts right now, not when there was a bit of journey left to enjoy.

The time on the train had delivered adventure and discoveries, along with enough dirt coming in through the windows to add a whole new state to the Union.

At last, the train came to a full stop. Wheels scraped the iron tracks, creating a high-pitch sound that made everyone grit their teeth. The children lunged forward in their seats from the sudden stop.

Then, on down the steps the children went, restless to get off, anxious to relieve themselves, and ready to wash in the stream. When the last one exited, Ruby grabbed hold of the railing with both hands and hobbled down the steps, all the while wishing she had her cane. When her feet touched the ground, she headed across the field, complaining about the uneven terrain.

Even after she relieved herself privately behind a tree, Ruby remained anxious. There was excitement afoot with the younger children, while she only tasted her unknown future. This was the last time they all would be together like this, a rag-tag family of sorts, having spent months so close together. It was obvious the openness of the prairie put everyone in good spirits, but soon a family would pick each of them like flowers for their home, the children having no say in the matter. Only Ruby felt in control of her own destiny, and she knew it was time for Red to be in control of his as well.

There was Andy, off yonder at the river bank, pulling a large, sturdy-looking stick. He walked toward Ruby, dragging the stick behind to offer it. "This will help you, Ruby."

She gave him a smile and leaned against the stick. Together, they walked into the shade of an old oak where they sat worshipful beneath the branches, overwhelmed by the solemnness of the moment.

Ruby retrieved the jar from her pocket and held it up. Ruby and Andy looked through the glass to see Red's antennae sweeping back and forth. Together, they unscrewed the lid on the jar for the very last time. Her red gem was about to be the first of the train riders to find a new home.

"This is the perfect place for Red. He has trees to climb, grass to run in, and a stream over there to drink from," Andy prodded.

Ruby nodded her head. She turned the jar on its side and waited for Red to scamper out. He walked to the edge and paused, his little whisker's flailing about. As if testing the grass, he walked out half way. Then, he ran for it as though he were escaping. Across the grass, over freshly fallen leaves, and up through the crevices of the nearest tree.

"I knew he'd like fresh air! Run free, Red!" Andy jumped in the air.

Attracted by their private actions, Louie watched with great interest. He came closer and sneered. "Dumb roach." In a single motion, Louie pressed his forefinger into the insect's back. There was a snap. The small creature's white innards squeezed out his sides.

"No!" Ruby released a blood-curling scream.

"Murderer!" Andy bawled and furiously kicked Louie in his legs. A good two feet taller, Louie shoved Andy down and walked away laughing.

Having kept it all this time, Ruby reached into her pocket and withdrew the same piece of wood Louie had used on her in the city. She gimped toward him, her arm raised, holding the wood. Louie howled with laughter and moved fast. There was no way she could keep up with him, but she kept trying anyway. Ruby was just feet behind him when her foot caught in a mouse hole. She tumbled down the embankment where she landed face down.

Ruby couldn't see through her tears. Her heart pounded with grief, and she struggled to breathe between deep sobs. Finally, Ruby pushed herself to a sitting position and found Andy kneeling next to her. "Red helped me through such lonely times. And now he's gone."

Andy calmed Ruby by gently patting her shoulder. "I bet we can find another bug. How do you feel about ladybugs? I know, a grasshopper! They jump really high like I do! We can name him—let's see—how about Andy, after me? I think it's a good name. What about you? Do you think Andy is a good name for your new pet?"

"Andy is a good name. I'm not ready for a new pet, though. It wouldn't be the same. I need time to mourn. Red was special. Matchless. I can't move on. My heart needs time to heal." She patted her chest.

Andy cupped his hand over his brows to shield his eyes from the penetrating sunshine. "I'm trying to see Red's ghost floating around up there."

Ruby wasn't ready to look. She picked up the wood and put it back into her pocket. Andy helped her stand and walk over to the stream's edge; then Andy plunged right into the water.

Andy acted witless springing about in it, splashing everyone. Momentarily forgetting her grief, she laughed at him, watching as he leaped and twirled, sending water swirls up into the air. He stopped moving and screamed out, "Watch out Ruby!"

Before she could turn, Ruby was grabbed from behind. Fingers pressed the nape of her neck and shoved her face under the water. Ruby frantically flailed her arms, trying to escape the unrelenting hold. Louie pushed her face to the bottom of the stream. Her last breath spent, she began to gulp water. His hands abruptly released, allowing her to jerk upward.

Louie now stood directly in front of her with his fists fixed up in the air. He clenched his mouth tightly which caused Ruby to think his jawbone might pop out of his mouth. Not able to run, she began vomiting water and mud.

"You leave Ruby alone! You leave her alone, you assassin! Assassinator of Red! Isn't one death enough for you?" Andy bawled. In one giant, death-defying leap, Andy saddled himself onto the back of the large teen. Fearlessly, Andy kicked and punched Louie from all angles. The older boy dug his dirty nails into Andy while spinning about, doing everything in his power to get the kid off his back. But wee Andy held on as though he were riding a wild horse.

Miss Claire and Miss Anna splashed through the shallows of the stream. Each woman tried to separate the boys and took their share of kicks.

Ruby now joined back in and pummeled Louie with her fists. The train conductor jumped from the coach car. He had no trouble with the terrain, crossing it in an instant.

The large man first grabbed Ruby and flung her ashore. Then, he worked to insert himself between Andy and Louie. Finally, he loosened Andy's grip, but Louie propelled Andy and the conductor backward. The conductor landed on his backside with Andy on top of him.

Not willing to give up, Miss Claire and Miss Anna finally pulled an exhausted Louie from the stream. Standing wet, tired, and bruised from being whooped by a kid half his age, Louie was clearly defeated; Ruby didn't think he looked so tough anymore. Even the little children began to tease him. The conductor, who was not happy with his unexpected dunking, did his best to cover a smile.

"What do you want me to do with him?" The conductor held him by the scruff of his neck.

"I think his public humiliation is enough, don't you agree, Miss Claire?"

"Yes, Miss Anna. I'm certain he will behave from here on out."

"You may be forgiving ladies, but something tells me that as soon as this young man gets a second wind, he'll be after the children again. For everyone's safety, he should be tied into his seat at least until the next stop." Louie hung his head as the conductor walked him back to the train. Gales of laughter continued in taunting cries.

"Ha! He deserves everything bad that comes his way," Ruby said. She then took a moment to dig bog from her teeth and gums and wrung water from the bottom of her dress.

"I saved your life, didn't I?" Andy beamed with happiness. "I saved you from drowning, and I don't even know how to swim! How d'you like that!"

"Thanks, Andy." She ruffled his red hair.

"Louie ain't so tough. I'm the tough one!" Little Andy pretended to flex muscles he didn't yet have.

After the children were all calmed, Miss Anna and Miss Claire distributed new clothes for a positive first impression to prospective parents. Ruby sat on the grass and helped pull off the children's old, worn, soiled clothes. For those in need of help, she tenderly slipped them into new clothes. Afterwards, she combed out hair, one head after the other. Ruby tended to everyone's appearance but her own.

Andy hid in the tall grass. Miss Anna spied him all the same. She rolled up her sleeves and dragged him back to the stream where she scrubbed him clean with a bar of soap. Given the druthers of a five year old, Andy would have chosen to just put the new clothes over his old, but Miss Anna would have none of that. He was physically forced to change into fresh clothes despite his loud protests to the contrary. Upon his transformation, he demanded that his smelly clothes be returned, which of course did not happen.

The waifs returned to the train. Ruby was the last one to climb back on, pulling herself up each step while holding the railing with both hands. Then, she gave a long backwards gaze toward the tree where Red met his fate.

Ruby stood at the front of the compartment and watched Miss Anna and Miss Claire pin numbers onto every teen and child, including Emily and Amy. Andy, too. Even Louie got one. That despicable lunatic was about to be unleashed on some poor, unsuspecting family.

"Why aren't their names on the paper?" Ruby asked Miss Anna.

"Because the numbers are for record-keeping purposes."

"But the numbers make them seem unimportant," Ruby said.

"It will be fine, Ruby."

"You can pin my number right here on my collar."

"Ruby, we have been over this. You don't get a number. You get to go back to New York."

"It's not fair." Ruby crossed her arms against herself in protest. It was best to let them think what they wanted for now, but Ruby had other plans, and they didn't include the orphanage—or any place with the like of the Mrs. Stone or Mrs. Perkins. Ruby figured her indomitable spirit would surely guide her back into trouble when she refused to return to New York, but her heart would find a home in Denton, Texas, the last stop. By then, the women would be bone tired and not as attentive.

After all the numbers had been placed, Miss Anna asked Ruby to unwrap the wet bandages on her legs so she could look at them. "Do they still hurt?"

"Sometimes, yes, ma'am. Mainly when I'm tired and have had a long day standing."

"The bandages are filthy and wet. I don't have clean replacements." Miss Anna bit her lip as she thought of what to do. "Let's not wrap them again. Let's allow the air to get at them."

"Yes, ma'am." Ruby wanted to hide the scarring, but grief and embarrassment were useless because they wouldn't change a thing.

"Are your legs looking beautiful yet?" Andy crouched down to have a look.

"They'll never be beautiful. They are what they are."

"Remember what I told you about butterflies? They start out as little worms that people want to flatten. They eat lots of leaves and make gardeners cuss, but one day they grow beautiful wings and fly away on them." Andy illustrated by waving his arms up and down.

The engine roared, and the whistle blew. The children's commotion grew, and Ruby returned to her seat with Andy once again on her lap. Then, the train moved along the iron tracks, slowly at first but gradually picking up speed as coal black smoke billowed from the smokestack and sent a bit of soot wafting on the wind into the train cars. Each car rattled in turn as the train struggled to get up to speed. At this moment, the children, the adults, and the train knew that it was not heading simply to a destination, but was heading to destiny.

Caring for Andy made Ruby feel he belonged to her. He must have felt the same way.

"I'm glad I have you, Ruby, because my folks are dead. Same as yours," he said. "They died of the flu. What did yours die from?"

"My folks aren't dead! Not both of them anyway! My mother is searching the whole world to find me right this minute. One day, I'll turn a corner, and she'll be there, smiling at me and will say, 'There you are! I have been looking all over for you. Where on God's good earth did you run off to all those years ago?' And then she'll hold me in her arms and never let me go." Ruby drew her knees up under her chin and wrapped her arms around herself in a hug. "It's been a long time since I last saw her, though. A lot can happen in one day, and it's been years now. I hate to say it aloud, but maybe the reason Mother never found me is that she's dead." Ruby startled herself; it was the first time she had ever said those words. She wondered what caused her to say them when she had just taken the biggest risk of her life by getting on this train.

"Ruby, I'll be your family if you want me to be." Andy's eyes were stormy blue and pure with hope.

Maybe having someone whose hand she could hold onto meant more than finding someone she could hardly remember. "Yes, Andy, I do."

"Let's shake on it! That means it's a promise." He reached out his hand.

"A promise!" Ruby grabbed hold and shook.

"Then you don't have to think about your mother looking for you anymore. You have me, and I really have you."

Ruby laughed at his messy hair that refused to stay in place no matter how much Miss Claire brushed it. Patting his unruly mop, she smiled. Here sat her family, Ruby's family. Andy was someone to belong to.

15

Before long, they reached the first stop. Hope for a safe life washed over all the children, making them sparkle more than soap had.

On the other side of the Mississippi River, in a town whose name Ruby's couldn't pronounce, the children jumped off the train. Ruby peered out the open window.

"What's happening out there?" called a muffled wee voice.

Realizing that Andy had not said his goodbyes, Ruby looked down to see him scrunched beneath a seat. "What are you doing under there? Don't you want a family?"

"Huh? I have a family: you. We shook on it, remember?"

"I remember," Ruby said, but she knew this reasoning would never hold up with Miss Claire or Miss Anna.

However, his words warmed her all up on the insides, enough so that she could have stood in snow up to her arm pits and not felt cold. Ruby was pleased he wanted to stay with her. With him, she didn't miss Red as much. She still cringed when she remembered Red's demise—being smashed into the tree with his white guts hanging out every which way. Today with Andy, she had a family, a family in the form of a freckle-faced little boy. The memory of this single day would have to last her forever. He could only escape Miss Claire's notice for a short time. After all, he was the only red-headed boy. Ruby looked out the window some more.

"What's happening?" Andy lay on his stomach and pushed up on his hands to see better.

"Lots of people out there! The children are lined up in rows, and people are looking over them from head to toe. One man is looking inside someone's mouth! How do my teeth look to you?" With teeth clenched and lips spread open, she showed her toothiest smile to Andy.

"Those are fine looking teeth! No food stuck in them either."

Ruby turned back to the window.

"What's happening now?" Andy whispered from his hiding place.

"Lots of children are being taken away by grownups. A couple of the bigger boys are leaving with men who are dressed in dirty clothes, just like the men look who work in city factories."

"Maybe they're farmers. Has anyone picked Louie?"

"Nope."

"Figures. Anyone look kind?"

Andy held her gaze in a way that went far beyond any words he could speak. It that moment, Ruby knew Andy needed a whole family. A family that included a mother and a father. She turned back to the window.

"Hard to tell for sure, but I think so. Some are laughing, and the children with numbers 1, 17, 39, and 24 are smiling big smiles." Ruby moved back and forth between the seats, to get a better look. Now she knew what a caged bird yearning to fly free felt like. Now she knew what Red felt like in his jar.

"Are they a family now?" asked Andy.

"I guess so."

"It can happen fast, just like us."

Ruby noticed an older couple talking to the blonde twin girls, numbers 3 and 4. In a few minutes, they chose only one of them, Amy, leaving the other, Emily. The sisters, who were about Ruby's age, began to cry. They reached out and clung to one another. The man and woman appeared very angry. They started walking away from both girls. Miss Claire intervened and held Emily back, while the woman grabbed at Amy's hand and pulled her away. Emily fell to the ground at Miss Claire's feet and sobbed. In a short moment, one a family had been destroyed in the name of creating another family.

Ruby wondered how anybody could decide which twin to take. How could Miss Claire allow them to split up the twins like that? And why would anyone even think of only taking one when they were like bookends holding up a shelf—thriving in pairs and lost by themselves? Twins were already a God-made family. Why undo it? Didn't they realize it would cause the girls to collapse and everything spill out? Undoing an existing family was wrong.

Ruby turned to tell Andy her opinion but instead pursed her lips together when she saw him dozing off to sleep, hands folded together under his head for a pillow. The warmth of the afternoon left beads of sweat on his face as if he had been in the water again. She looked at her family.

If she could pick a younger brother from anyone in the world, it would be Andy.

Of all the children that had begun the train pilgrimage, most had already found homes. By late afternoon, children had been picked, papers had been signed, and everyone had left. It was time for the train to move on to the next town with people waiting along the tracks.

It was a bittersweet moment. This was the threshold of becoming a family that some lost and others never had. The children had been family to each other—fighting, playing, and eating together—but now each was to walk off with strangers who would raise them into adulthood. Some parents would be warm, like Mama and Papa Burke, while others would be cold and harsh like Mrs. Stone and Mrs. Perkins. And all along, the children had no choice. Some suffered goodbyes silently. Some hugged for the first time. Some cried inconsolably. But some were also happy.

The remaining children marched back up the train steps and into the thinly cushioned seats. Gone was the excitement that had effervesced hours earlier. Was it due to the pain or the relief of not being chosen? Now there was more than enough room for Andy to sit beside Ruby. Louie sat alone, tied back up, not uttering a sound. Just the same, Ruby kept one eye on him. The remaining twin, Emily, cried for her sister long into the night. All of Miss Claire's prayers and reasoning were not enough to soothe the hurt. When Emily's crying finally stopped, she sat lifeless with empty eyes, but she kept on breathing. She was a living ghost.

Images of the children in new homes with strangers now their kin ran through Ruby's mind. Were they sitting happily together with warm dinner on the table, or were they trembling in the darkness, sent to bed alone without goodnight prayers to watch over them? She both envied and pitied them. How many of their stories would have happy endings?

The remaining children sat with far-off gazes as they rode above the massive steel wheels that screeched along the long shiny rails. As the Orphan Train made its way further south and west, each child was lost in their own daydreams spawned by the rhythm of the coach car's bounces. All were emotionally drained. They sat on the edge of their futures, like it or not. Eventually, each settled into private, subdued stupors.

16

The Orphan Train had three stops left. Three chances for a family and three chances to be rejected. Chances for siblings to be separated and chances for the hooligans to be chosen.

The first two stops were identical with children stomping off the train in clean clothes, dusty shoes, and apprehensive hearts. Each time, they wore numbers pinned to their clothes. Adults crowded about them, pushing and shoving. Some felt the muscles on teenage boys, while others spoke softly and wiped away frightened tears. An argument broke out between two sets of parents who wanted the same child, as if he were a Christmas doll to be fought over. A couple picked the remaining twin, Emily. She walked off with them in a haze. Perhaps she would see Amy again one day when they were grown-up women.

As the train continued to the last stop, Andy scooted forward from under the seat, and Miss Anna laid a squinty eye on him. She took hold of him by the scruff of his neck.

"There you are!" She crowed. "You are not hiding from me again. Not this time. Denton, Texas is our last stop, and you will get off this train, like it or not!"

"Not! Not!" Andy twisted himself this way and that, trying to wriggle out of her clutch.

Miss Anna tried to pin a number on his shirt, but he would have no part of it. Miss Anna couldn't get the job done. "Ruby, help me."

Without hesitation, Ruby hoisted herself up and took hold of Andy's arms while Miss Anna held him in place between her knees. Andy was now number 46. He was no longer a little boy filled with liveliness but was instead reduced to a number drawn on paper.

Betrayal crossed Andy's face, a look Ruby had never before seen. Disbelief. Anger. Only his eyes moved as he searched Ruby's face, as though he needed an answer to his forthcoming question: "Ruby, you said we were family! Don't you want me anymore?" His shoulders slumped, and a little boy's panic took over. He began to tremble.

"Andy, I want you until the day I die." She tipped his face up so she could look at him.

"Thank you, Ruby, for your help. Be sure you remain on the train." Miss Anna pulled Andy toward the steps. A new burst of energy made him fight her harder until the conductor arrived to help.

"Ruby! Ruby! Save me! You promised! You said you'd never go back on a promise, remember?"

"I remember." She yelled, shaking her head and wiping tears from her face. She was tired of losing people in her life. There was no getting used to it.

Andy broke away and ran back into Ruby's arms, burying his face in her neck.

His sobs tore Ruby apart. All she could think about was keeping Andy for herself. Saying goodnight prayers together. Teaching him to read. Insisting he wear clean clothes. But none of it could happen. She knew it, and Andy was too young to know it. They both wanted what they couldn't have, and this was the moment of reckoning. Ruby gently held Andy at arm's length and looked into his little boy's eyes. She saw bewilderment in them.

"You have to go with Miss Anna and find yourself a family with a mother and a father who know how to take good care of you. Hear me? We can't be together no matter how hard we wish. Sometimes, things just ain't fair no matter how you slice it. But no matter how far apart we are, we will always be family. Someday, when I'm grown up and you're grown up, I'll come and find you."

The conductor picked up Andy, wrapping both his arms around the boy tightly to prevent another escape.

"You promised!" Andy looked angry and confused—his body stiff with rage. "You went back on your promise to me! You're still lying. You won't never come for me. I hate you, Ruby Red. I hate you!"

Ruby recoiled at his words. It was as though her heart dropped from her chest and left an empty place. Words had left her, too. Helplessly, Andy was physically removed from the train. Ruby said a silent daytime prayer that good people would sweep Andy into their hearts and carry him off in their arms of love—and that all that affection would make him forget her.

Ruby had only enough strength left to make it back to her seat where she opened the top window to welcome a cool breeze. Louie then caught her eye. He stood below a railroad sign that read "WELCOME TO DENTON."

For the second time in two days, Louie seemed weak and distressed, cowed. Once fearful of his size and fierceness, she now saw he was really just a scared boy about her age with a number pinned on his shirt. She was surprised to feel sorry for him.

A short, stout man talked to him for quite a while, along with what she guessed to be the man's wife, a remotely pleasant-looking woman. Ruby tried to hear what they said but couldn't make out the words. Then, she saw them all shake hands as if saying goodbye. Ruby bet she wouldn't be the only one in the train returning to New York with Miss Claire and Miss Anna. Louie would ride back, too. Ruby kept watching, a laugh crowning her lips, and nearly coughed in surprise when Louie walked off with the mild-looking young couple. They stood in line to sign papers for guardianship.

"Imagine that. Even Louie got himself a home. They'd better sleep with one eye open if they know what's good for them."

Ruby craned her neck around, trying to spot Andy. There he was, standing with his hands shoved into his pockets, a scowl on his face.

The train was nearly ready for its return trip. Just as she had decided her daring move to get onto the train in New York City, she now decided to make a daring move to get off the train in Denton, Texas. She had to make her move quickly, or else her chance would dance right on by.

The plan was simple: when everyone's attention was drawn someplace else, she'd get off and walk around the station building, disappearing into the tree line. No telling how far she could get before anyone noticed her missing. If they couldn't find her, they'd have to leave without her; the train could only sit idle on the tracks for so long.

Ruby remained seated, watching for a distraction. Everyone's back was to the train. People seemed occupied with meeting the children and signing papers for them. It was busy. More opportunities slipped right on by, but she couldn't leave Andy just yet. He looked so frightened.

And then, a harsh-looking, bosomy woman, with what appeared to be her skinny husband, tried speaking to Andy. But he'd have none of it. He kept his arms crossed, head bowed, and refused speak. They finally gave up and walked slowly back to their horse-drawn wagon.

A particular man caught Ruby's attention. He was angular-shaped, dressed in wrinkled clothes, and leaning against a dented, rusted-out truck. Just the sight of him gave her the willies. He made his move as soon as the other couple walked away, as if he had been waiting for his chance with Andy. Chills ran up Ruby's spine.

The man whistled. He held a heavy stick that he twirled with each step he took. Ruby noticed he was different from the other adults who spoke to the children first. Stickman didn't. He just walked up to Miss Anna and pointed at Andy. He wanted that particular boy for his own. "No, no, tell him no!" Ruby yelled through the open window, hitting the lower pane with her hand, but no one paid her any attention.

Miss Anna looked worried but reluctantly agreed and slowly put the papers together. One look at the man and

Andy let out a blood-curdling scream. He turned and ran toward the train.

"Rubeeee!"

Ruby sprang off the seat and moved as fast as she could down the aisle, but her shorter leg felt unduly stiff from all the recent train riding, causing her to be slower.

"I'm coming, Andy!" she hollered, praying he heard her. "Hang on! I'm coming!"

Halfway to the front, she stumbled and fell flat on her face. Ruby felt dizzy but shook herself out of it. She grabbed hold of a seat and pulled herself up on it. She had to keep moving. Andy was at the train door.

"Andy!" Ruby reached out her hand to him.

Andy reached back. They were inches apart when Stickman appeared. In a second, his hands were on Andy, who looked terrified as he was carried out of her sight.

"No! Andy! I'm coming for you, Andy!" Ruby worked her way to the door.

"You're a no-good, stinking pig!" Andy told Stickman.

Ruby held on to the railing with both hands and moved herself down the steep steps, trying not to fall, trying to hurry before Andy was taken away in that beat-up old truck. Why didn't Miss Anna or Miss Claire see in Stickman that she saw? Was a bad home really better than none at all?

At last, Ruby made it to the tracks just as Stickman backhanded Andy across his freckled face. The small boy fell like a lead pipe to the ground where he lay absolutely still. The man raised his foot and began to stomp on Andy's head and ribs. Miss Anna shrieked, and Miss Claire yelled for someone to get the police.

Ruby made her way to them and reached for the stick he beat Andy with, but she couldn't get hold of it, so she threw herself on top of Andy instead.

"Please, Mister! Don't hurt Andy anymore," Ruby pleaded. She felt the man's stick come down on the back of her head again and again. He hit her hard and fast. People shouted for him to stop, and finally, a man stepped from the pack and grabbed Stickman's arm.

"I wouldn't do that again if I were you." His eyes filled with fierce intensity as he twisted the stick away. "I'm Frank Bindle from the Denton Record News. We have a circulation of over 5,000, and my readers would love to hear how a grown man beat two helpless orphans, whose only prayers were to be taken in by loving families. I don't think any one of our readers will take kindly to that. What is your name and address, sir?" Frank broke the stick over his knee and then stood with his fist ready to swing at the bully's face.

Stickman backed away and ran to his truck. In a moment, the wheels kicked up dirt as they rolled over the road.

Ruby looked at the side of Andy's swollen face. She held his small hand with her own bloodied fingers, and dread filled her up on the inside.

Frank knelt beside Andy. He looked at Ruby and flinched; then he took a handkerchief from his back pocket. Folding it into fourths, he pressed it onto Ruby's forehead to stop her bleeding. "Are you alright?"

She couldn't answer; her mouth had turned to cotton. Blood spilled from the open wounds onto her blue dress.

He looked at her, his eyes serious and worried. The firm grasp of his hand ministered peace to her spirit. After a couple attempts to swallow, she finally spoke: "Can you help Andy?" She lifted a shaking hand to point at him.

"Of course." Frank carefully rolled Andy over onto his back. Andy looked like a wounded bird felled by a slingshot. Only a hint of breath remained inside of him.

Miss Claire and Miss Anna hurried to them carrying wet towels and quickly began to wash Andy's face. They called his name and prayed aloud to Jesus to wake him up. As a second thought, Miss Anna checked Ruby and asked how she was feeling. Ruby didn't answer; it was plain to anyone with good eyesight that she was fine save for a few bloody wounds. It was her heart that had broken.

"This boy doesn't look right to me; he isn't responding." Frank's eyes darted from face to face. "He needs medical attention. My truck is parked behind the station. We can use that to take him to the hospital."

"Should we take Ruby, too?" Miss Claire asked.

"No, I'll be fine here." Ruby scooted back.

"Ruby, come with us," Frank insisted.

"No." Ruby eyed the trees. It was now or never to make her escape.

"Okay, but you wait right here for us. We'll be back as soon as we can. I will tell the conductor. Don't leave," Miss Claire said.

Ruby sat on the station's porch and watched Frank carry Andy away. His limbs bounced around like a ragdolls as he was placed into the back with Miss Anna. Miss Claire got into the front and quickly slammed the door shut like she was in a big hurry and there was no time to close it softly. The truck pulled out and disappeared down the street. Ruby looked around at the empty train and station. Good or bad, every other child had found a home. Only the conductor and the train master remained inside the station with the door closed. This was her moment. By the time everyone retuned, there'd be no telling which way Ruby had gone. They'd have to leave without her.

Ruby started toward the woods on uneven ground. With her mind on Andy, she kept picturing him hurt. Why didn't she say she wanted to go to the hospital, too? That way she could have kept an eye on him. No one knew Andy like she did. As she reconsidered her decision to leave before knowing Andy's outcome, she tripped. It wasn't enough to cause her to fall, but the stumble jerked her body. Now her hip ached. Within yards of the woods, she could easily disappear into them within minutes. Ruby turned to face the station, torn between freedom and Andy. With her head down, feeling defeated but knowing it was the right thing to do, she returned to the station where she sat alone, waiting for news.

Ruby looked at her fingers and thought about things she had learned on her journey here with Andy. Here, they were in the Promised Land together, yet Andy might be shaking hands with Death this very moment, on his way to crossing over. If so, he could meet Papa Burke and Red in Heaven. Maybe her mother was there, too. That is, if they had all gone on to their great reward, which Ruby was not sure was a fact. But if indeed Papa Burke and her mother and Red had, her mother would look at Andy and say, "There you are! A fine looking boy you are and friend of my Ruby's to boot. I heard you two decided you were family. Please sit a while and tell me about how our girl is doing. I have missed her so much."

It was quiet as a graveyard, but then she heard the truck returning. There was an eerie heaviness on everyone's face as Miss Anna and Miss Claire and Frank got out of the car. Ruby waited to see Andy. But then they closed the doors. Andy wasn't with them. The late afternoon sun cast odd shadows as they walked toward the station. There was no breeze in the air to lift the humidity. Frank slowed his pace.

Ruby was sure then that Andy was dead.

17

At first, no one noticed her leave. Ruby's heart picked up speed as she headed back toward the tree line. No way could anyone stop her now. She was done with death. Tired of losing people and pets she loved. There'd be no more of it. No matter how many people called to her, she wouldn't stop. She kept walking. Kept going. She'd go as fast as she could manage until her legs could take her no further. Then she'd lay down and ask God to let her cross over too.

Frank easily caught up to Ruby and took her by the shoulders to steady her. His breath came in gasps. "Andy is in tough shape, but he's at the hospital."

By then, Miss Anna had caught up to them as well. Out of breath, she patted her chest, as if trying to beat air back into her lungs. "Ruby, don't run off like that. I have good news for you. Andy has a wonderful home. This fine gentleman is taking him. I know that will make you happy."

"Maybe. If you're the right sort who will be good to him, then I will be happy."

"Ruby, of course he will be good to him," Miss Anna explained. "Mr. Bindle, I apologize for Ruby's rudeness."

"It's alright. She's scared."

Ruby looked the man up and down. His hair was the color of city brick. Aside from the crook in his nose, he seemed nice enough. His appearance didn't leave much to complain about because his clothes were clean and so were his fingernails. Still, there were certain people who could act one way at one moment and then be totally different in another moment, like Mrs. Stone. She had clean fingernails, too, and when company was present, her voice was soft and so kind when she spoke to Mama and Papa Burke. But after the visitors left, her manner became most sharp and ugly. And at this point in time, Ruby didn't fully trust anyone. Life had taught her to be careful. No snap judgement. People had to prove themselves over time.

Despite the news about Andy, Ruby was overcome with sadness. Now that Andy was staying, Miss Anna and Miss Claire would supervise Ruby's every move. Ruby looked up at the blemish-free sky. However long it took to get back to New York, it would not be long enough. There was countryside to take in, the tune of birds to hear along the way, and prairie flowers to admire. And there'd always be Andy to think about. She was sure remember everything from their short time together for the rest of her life. She might even draw it out on a tablet if she ever got another one.

Ruby handed the gentleman's handkerchief back to him. "Sorry there's blood on it. I can try to wash some of it off in the station's bathroom, if you'd like."

"No, Ruby." Miss Anna stepped in. "We're not letting you out of our sight again."

"It's not necessary." Frank stuffed it into the back pocket of his pants.

They walked back to the station together where Frank signed the papers to become Andy's legal guardian. Ruby drew a picture with her index finger in the dirt. It caught Frank's attention.

"What's that you're drawing?"

"Sir?"

"I see you're drawing something in the dirt. I was wondering about it."

Was he mad at her? Had she done or said something that was ill mannered? Ah, this is the other side of him. She knew it was just a matter of time until the other shoe dropped.

"Answer him, Ruby," Miss Claire instructed her. "You are being discourteous."

"It's just a picture of trees and a house, sir." She held his gaze.

"Oh, then this is your house?" he asked.

"I have no house." Her stomach tied in knots. It wasn't a comforting feeling.

"I can tell that you and Andy are good friends." He smiled, but he made her jittery. She lowered her eyes. "You care about each other." His voice was kind, though.

Ruby squinted her eyes against the blaze of the hot afternoon sun. Perspiration beaded at the man's forehead and ran into the folds of his neck. She felt guilty for getting her blood all over the handkerchief because it looked like he could use a clean one.

"If I could be family with anyone, it would be with Andy. You'll like him." She stared at her picture.

Frank turned to Miss Anna. "What a delightful young girl. Tell me about her."

"Ruby is a strong-willed child who is also orphaned."

"I have an indomitable spirit."

"I see that." Frank laughed. "My folks used to say the same thing about me when I was a boy."

Miss Anna walked up behind Ruby and touched her hair with affection. "Just to show you how strong-willed she is, she snuck onto the train. We're taking her back to New York. And we will see that she gets a position in a good house. Didn't she just have an offer, Miss Claire?"

"Yes, she did. But it wasn't quite right for her, so we are still looking."

"If no one has legal claim to her, I'd like to take guardianship of her as well as Andy."

"Ruby?"

"Me?"

"Yes, but the decision is really up to you, Ruby. What do you want?" Frank touched her shoulder.

Ruby placed her hands behind her. Filled with fear, she couldn't answer. Why was this white man touching her dark skin? What would he want with a gimpy servant? He already got a happy red-headed boy. Maybe he was tricking her. He wanted to see her get her hopes up and then snatch it away again.

"Before you decide, there is something you need to see." Miss Anna pulled up Ruby's skirt, revealing the burned skin and twisted knee. Ruby knew that would do it. At least she had her pick of train seats for the ride back to New York City.

Frank knelt and asked, "What happened?" His eyes looked so sad she wanted to cry.

"Spilled hot grease on them, sir." She furrowed her brow at him. No mention of frying them. Neither did she cross her eyes. For once, she offered the truth.

"I'm very sorry."

Ruby looked at him as though he were strange bug.

"I'm frequently on the road traveling for my newspaper. Maybe you've heard of it? The Denton Record?"

"If you say so." Ruby squinted at him.

"Forgive me, I'm feeling a little nervous here." He heaved a sigh and began again, "I just got married about a year ago to a wonderful Italian woman. Marie, that's my wife, complains about how lonely she is when I'm gone. She just stays in the house, isolating herself from everyone, and I thought if we had children—we've talked about having children—but I'm quite a bit older than she is." Frank kept trying to pin down his words, "So, I thought when Andy gets out of the hospital, it would be nice if you were there, too. The way I see it, if Marie has you both to look after, she won't be so lonely when I'm gone. It's up to you, Ruby. It's your decision to make. You decide if you want to come live with Andy, Marie, and me. Yes or no?"

Ruby rolled her eyes in thought and then looked him up and down. Her first daring move had been when she hopped on the train. This would be her second daring move of the week. "What if I can't do a pleasing job of it?"

"I have faith in you, Ruby."

"Then I decide yes. I can look after them both, Mr. Bindle."

"Two things, Ruby. First of all, call me Frank." He bit his lower lip. "And secondly, Ruby, my wife will look after you and Andy."

"You want her to look after me, not me look after her?" Ruby cocked her head to one side trying to sort it out. "I'm not sure how to do that, Mr. Frank."

"I'm not sure how taking care of children works either, but we can figure it all out together. I'm sure Marie will have her own ideas; she always does." Frank laughed as he signed papers to be Ruby's guardian. "Are you ready to go home with me, Ruby?"

When she didn't answer, he held out his hand to her.

Her heart beat so fast she heard it in her ears. Ruby walked over to Frank with an awkward step, her stomach tumbling. She gulped hard—and took his white hand.

18
. . . . .
Denton, Texas: population 8,000

Frank whistled a bit as he drove. It wasn't at all comforting. In fact, she found it annoying and set her teeth on edge. Ruby studied the profile of this stranger. A long nose that came to a point, almost like a bird's beak. Thin lips matched his angular face, although his chin jutted out too much for him to be called handsome. His thick brown hair, with streaks of gray, showed signs of a fresh cut.

Beads of perspiration ran down her face and neck as she took it all in. Wood and brick shops formed a square around a sandstone courthouse that sat in the middle of four dirt streets. Much smaller than New York City—Denton was like a speck on a fat man's skin.

"What do you think, Ruby? How does it look to you?"

"Looks fine."

"I think getting used to a new place can be hard. Give it time."

"I'll do that, Mr. Frank."

As they turned right, Ruby read the street sign: McKinney. It was important to know how to get back and forth from town in case she needed to do shopping for the missus of the mansion. Memorization was essential. Ruby was good at that.

From what she could tell, though small, the town would suit her just fine. She was smiling away when she spotted a most disturbing sight that made her want to run back to the woods and never come back out. Just before the Bell Street sign. A crowd of dark-skinned people were making a racket—shouts of despair and deep-rooted travails. A large house sat amid the shanties which she guessed were their homes. Families carried boxes of belongings to wagons, while others just piled them on the curb and looked around for some way to cart them off. Women pulled down clothes lines still strung with garments. Tears of misery ran down faces. Snotty-nosed children hollered for their mamas. The sight, sounds, and odors were so overwhelming that Ruby wondered what she had gotten herself into by agreeing to go with this Mr. Frank. She looked hard at him again, wondering what kind of a man she was riding next to. Having been so caught up in what seemed like a brand new life, she had let down her guard.

Ruby wanted to plug her ears. Close her eyes. Crawl in a ball. Somehow, she knew it was important for her to watch this sight. She got to her knees and leaned halfway out the window to watch the misery. A large black man took a long look at Ruby sitting in the truck next to Frank. He narrowed his eyes. Ruby felt ashamed, as though she needed to be in the dirt helping and not riding with a white man. If only she could get out of the truck and assist with the packing and hauling, but she was too frightened to move.

Frank slowed the truck. "It's a sad day for these fine folk."

"Mr. Frank, did the missus of that splendid house tell her servants to leave?" Her hands trembled. Her heart hurt so bad she thought it just might break. The stench of raw sewage stirred her stomach. She covered her mouth and breathed into her hands, trying to keep from messing up the truck. The noise and cries of people wailing was mesmerizing, and she felt as though she had gone from the fry pan straight into the fire. It was too awful to see, yet she couldn't turn away. The image burned.

"That's not a house. The large building you see is a hotel. It's being torn down along with the houses."

Ruby sat without stirring as Mr. Frank pulled the truck to the side of the road and took out a small spiral notebook and a pencil. He watched the sorrow on Bell Street and then wrote.

Ruby shook her head. "Where will they all go?"

"Some are moving to a place called Solomon Hill, a few miles from here."

"What about the others? Where will they go?"

"I don't know, Ruby. Some have already left town."

"Did they do something wrong?" Ruby remembered the Christmas doll.

"There's an adult explanation for what is happening, but I can't explain it to you because I don't understand it myself. Some people are just fearful, Ruby, and it makes them do things that they can never be proud of. No, these people did nothing wrong."

Ruby sank back into the seat, thinking she landed in a worse place than New York.

19

Ruby stood in front of the small two-story gray house. It wasn't a mansion, yet she suddenly wanted it to belong to her.

The small dwelling sat on a street without sidewalks in the front. A huge cornfield beckoned to her around back from the squeaking screen door. Flowers bloomed like colorful flames everywhere in the garden. In fact, the house looked as though it had sprung from a special seed. Standing on this side of the front door, Ruby knew its insides would be filled with magic and love, that it had special transforming powers to change her into the person she was supposed to be—that is, if she stayed long enough for that to happen.

Frank turned the knob and opened the door. Ruby hopped over the threshold, knowing her old struggles lay behind her and better days lay ahead.

Where she stood in the hallway, she could see into all the rooms on the first floor. Yes, these people needed her. The place was in terrible disarray; it was obvious they had been without a maid for a very long time. Good thing Frank picked her. She knew right then he was a smart man for doing so.

Walking through the parlor, Ruby got a whiff of paint and turpentine. There were stacks of large paper held together by metal spiral loops. A canvas held an image of a prairie starflower, vigorous in new bloom. Piles of newsprint were heaped in corners, folded clothes were strewn across the couch, and furniture was set at odd angles.

Ruby stepped around furniture as she trailed behind Mr. Frank, past vases filled with prairie flowers, through the dining room and into the kitchen where the counters and table were lined with more vases stuffed with more flowers. Frank saw Ruby staring at the flowers. He pointed to each flower and called it by name: "Mexican hat, Indian mallow, Lantana, Milkweed, and Prairie paintbrush."

Ruby committed each flower to memory. They seemed important somehow.

"Stay behind me," Frank whispered and winked mischievously. The screen door opened with a whine of complaint. In the backyard, a lovely but mysterious woman painted cornfields as a blanket with fringe made of golden tassels of hair.

"Hi, honey. I have a surprise for you!" By the sound of his voice, Ruby knew Mr. Frank loved her very much.

"What? Are those more flowers behind your back?" She put her right hand on her hip and laughed. "If so, I don't know where I'm going to put them!"

"No flowers this time. Something so much better. Come on out, Ruby," Frank said. Timid, Ruby crept from behind and stood shivering in the sunlight. "Marie, I'd like you to meet our new houseguest, Ruby."

The first thing Ruby noticed was Marie's mouth dropping

wide open. Her hair was the color of midnight sky, and it fell down her back like a stream. Her eyes were violet. A pale orange cotton dress came down to her ankles, and she seemed comfortable wearing nothing on her feet. That's when Ruby noticed red paint on her toenails. It made her gasp with delight.

She searched the woman's face for a bit of welcoming, but it was a few minutes in coming. Marie slowly wiped her brush on a rag. That done, she chose another brush to wipe and then another. Ruby figured she needed an adjustment time to figure out what needed to be said at a moment like this. When all the brushes had been properly wiped, Marie said, "Hello there, Ruby. I'm Marie." She extended her hand to shake.

Ruby kept her arms rigidly at her sides.

"Don't be afraid." Marie pressed her hand out farther.

The request wasn't in the words, but in the treatment of saying the words. Right away Ruby sensed a goodness in the young woman that went right through her olive-colored skin and into her heart. Changing her mind, she took a chance and held out her hand, too, and shook Marie's.

"Come on, let's go into the kitchen. I bet you're hungry, am I right?"

Back inside the gray house, Frank asked Ruby to take a seat, and he removed two vases of dead flowers from the kitchen table and set them on the counter. It seemed odd he didn't toss them. Marie pulled the cookie jar from the Sellers kitchen cabinet and a pint of milk from the icebox and set them both down in front of Ruby.

"Help yourself. We'll be right back."

She took Frank's hand and led him out the back door where they could talk out of earshot. Ruby took the lid off the jar and reached in for the cookies. They were perfectly round and chock-full of chocolate chunks and walnuts. She shoved them one by one into her mouth. Marie had been right about Ruby being hungry.

What words could Frank use that would explain Ruby to his wife? Who'd have thought he'd bring a black girl home on this sunny summer day? Certainly not Marie. She was expecting more flowers. Ruby shrugged her shoulders, took another huge bite of cookie, and dribbled milk down her front when she went for a sip. Her stomach began to churn a bit; she ate more slowly and watched the couple through the window.

Frank rubbed the back of his neck and stared down at his feet. He reminded her of Papa Burke just then. It was the same pose Papa Burke struck anytime he was upset, so she figured this was how Mr. Frank was feeling, too: upset.

Then their voices hushed. Marie gave a backwards look at Ruby through the window, and they walked out of sight. Ruby could only hear the sound of footsteps on the porch followed by a long stretch of silence. Eventually, she heard the front door creak open and shut.

"Let me tell her, Frank."

Never knowing what the rest of the day could bring, Ruby put a few cookies into her pockets. If they were sending her away, hopefully it'd happen after dinner. A full stomach would be most welcome before facing another new future.

20

Marie walked back into the kitchen. Her bare feet slapped loudly against the linoleum floor. She smiled softly when she saw Ruby's perplexed expression.

"Come here, dear."

Heart thumping recklessly, Ruby slid out of her chair ready to swear an oath she hadn't stolen one thing in their absence. Then she remembered the cookies in her pocket. It frightened her to her bones. But she wasn't all that sure if that would be considered stealing since Marie told her to help herself.

Marie looked at her long and hard. Then she started flinging open cabinets filled with every kind of canning Ruby could imagine. "Here, we have peaches and sliced apples. Jars of sweet pickles, stewed tomatoes, green beans, and corn." Marie jerked on the silver handle on the icebox hard making the glass milk bottles rattle. Inside was a fat ham taking up space and a pitcher of orange juice with real slices of oranges floating right on the top of it. Even a hunk of Swiss cheese wrapped in wax paper had its own compartment. Marie slid open a drawer, and it was filled to the brim with chocolate bars.

"Wow."

"Ruby, anything you want to eat, you can have. Choose things that make you happy when you eat them. You need some fattening up." Then she held out her hand to the girl. "Come on, I want to show you to your room."

"Did you say *my* room?" Eyes wide with amazement, Ruby felt electrocuted again—only this time with joy. She could barely make her legs move forward as she held onto the wooden railing and slowly followed Marie up the soft carpeted stairway into a room under the eaves at the front of the house. Wind blew the lace curtains from the open window. Sunlight filtered through the lace to project shifting patterns on the floor. A clean patchwork quilt was spread across the iron bed. The wallpaper featured fat yellow roses in various stages of flowering. A dresser stood in the corner with a small rocking chair close by. Every bit of it was meant for her. She stood in disbelief; then, feeling a bit faint, she sat down.

"This is my room?"

It was just the sort of room she'd be warm and happy in until she was laid to rest. Myna was right about God leading her home. "Surely goodness and mercy followed me here."

"When Andy gets out of the hospital, he'll have the room across the hall. Come and look." Marie grabbed Ruby's hand and hurried across the hall.

"What do you think, Ruby? Will Andy be pleased?" Marie asked, leaning against wallpaper with blue sailboats. A small bed was angled in the corner with a tiny bedside table next to it, a large trunk at the foot. The room was shady with an oak tree growing right outside the window.

Birds chirped from a nest resting in the crux of a branch.

"He will like this fine!" Ruby nodded her head.

"Frank's and my room is at the end of the hall," Marie said, holding on to Ruby's hand again and hurrying down the hall. "If you need us any time of the night, come and wake us up."

Ruby stopped short of stepping on the rug. This bedroom was the largest of the three but not by much. The brass bed was covered with needlepoint pillows. Two matching dressers with mirrors, a large desk with a lamp and chair, and an overstuffed chair next to the window completed the room's furnishings. The walls were painted a tranquil shade of light green. Scattered rugs lay on the pine-planked floor. Ruby heard the loud tick of a wind-up alarm clock from a dresser top. How anyone could sleep with the constant racket? It'd be a hard chore moving about all that furniture to clean behind, but suddenly she didn't mind. She found herself liking these people.

Surely she'd landed right in the middle of a straight road that Mama Burke said was in Little Orphan Annie. How she wished Mama and Papa Burke and Myna could see her right now, staying clear up on the second floor in her very own room! It was worth getting a few whacks on the head to be here.

"Tomorrow, we'll buy you some new clothes. Maybe you can help me pick out some things for Andy, too. I don't know anything about him, so you will have to tell me." Marie said.

By the time they returned to the kitchen, Frank had made sandwiches from thick slices of bread with ham, cheese, and pickles, and he'd poured three tall glasses of cold orange juice.

"Too hot to cook," he said, smiling.

"I could have made those for you." Ruby fretted that she appeared lazy.

"Frank made them. And he's also right about the weather. It's hot in this house. Let's eat on the front porch where there's an evening breeze stirring. Everyone pick up your plates and follow me!"

"Ma'am, if you will just show me to the trays, I can tote them for you. My legs look a mess, and I do limp a bit, but I'm very strong. And given time, I promise not to spill."

"At this house, we all carry our own plates and drinks. And we clean up our own spills, don't we Frank?"

"That we do."

Marie and Frank sat on metal chairs, but Ruby felt more comfortable sitting a few feet away from them on the wooden steps. Her stomach was calm, but her mind stirred. Ruby had never been treated this way. She wasn't used to it. *They don't need me here. They just want me here.* Ruby was confused. It was hard to trust when there had never been any opportunity to do it before. She had no experience with it. Nonetheless, it was a good feeling.

"Dear Lord, thank you for steering Ruby our way. Bless her and may she feel at home here. Bless this food. Amen."

With one eye shut and the other eye fixed on the couple, Ruby studied their faces. No one had ever used the words "bless" and "Ruby" in the same sentence during her entire life.

She decided Marie and Frank must be brimmed full of goodness to care about these things, but still, she couldn't shake the thought that there must be a nasty surprise heading at full speed right toward her. If only she could be safe and trust what was right in front of her without worrying about tomorrow. Even so, it was obvious these people had no idea what her place was or how to treat her. She didn't mind.

After the porch talk had stopped, the cool evening breeze began. Ruby followed the couple back inside the house where Marie washed and rinsed the dishes in the cast iron sink, and Ruby dried. Now her innards quaked, so she kept a watch out on the couple from the corner of her eye. Never before this miracle day had she ever seen a white person lift a hand to do any kind of work—that is except for Miss Anna and Miss Claire.

Frank and Marie tucked her in with goodnight prayers. As she lay in bed that night, she heard the whistle of a train and thought of Andy sleeping in the hospital. She thought of Papa Burke lying in Pauper's Cemetery and Mama Burke standing up cooking at the Stone house. She thought about Myna telling someone new about prayers. Then she thought of Louie who was much closer than she liked. For the first night in a very long time, thoughts of her mother never entered her mind. She fell asleep with jaws sore from grinning.

21

Ruby awoke to the sound of birds flapping in the trees. The sun spread across the bed, filling the room with a warm glow. After dressing, she tiptoed down the hall to Mr. Frank and Mrs. Marie's bedroom to begin her work. The night before, Frank had snored so powerfully that Ruby was sure the windowpanes had cracked, but when she checked them, they were just fine.

The bed was already neatly made up with the top blanket tucked around the edges. Even the sleeping clothes were neatly hung on the closet hooks. Her heart sank. Already, she was slipping up. From here on out, she'd be up before dawn. Creeping past the bathroom, she heard Frank singing as he splashed in the tub. Ruby covered her mouth to keep from laughing out loud. Then, down the steps she went and out the back door to see Marie at her work.

It seemed natural watching Marie tinker with paint jars in the dappled shade of the giant oak. There seemed to be stories locked up inside of her head that she was only willing to talk about on her canvases. Marie had painted the wind as if an invisible child had run through the grass, squashing the blades down, chasing the wind into a field of corn and then up into the clouds.

Ruby left Marie alone with the beauty of her work and set to making breakfast on the stove, already hot with fire. Ruby set a black iron skillet on a burner and placed slabs of bacon into neat rows. When they curled and turned dark, Ruby used a fork to pull them out. Next, Ruby broke open the shells of brown eggs and let the innards drip down into the pan. Just as they spit and sizzled a bit, Frank walked in pulling up his trouser suspenders. She smiled and stepped aside to show him the pan. It was then she noticed the most unappetizing sight of dried blood on her dress, so she quickly bent to the side to hide the spots.

"What are you doing?" Frank asked, snatching the spatula out of her hand.

"I couldn't find an apron, sir." Ruby backed up until she bumped into the wall.

"That's not what I mean. I didn't bring you here so you could cook for us." Frank ran his fingers through his hair.

"I'm sorry. I— I just don't know the right thing to do. Please tell me what that is," she begged, tears filling her eyes. She patted her pockets. The cookies were there. The train was gone.

"Ruby?" Frank looked at her confused, and his voice softened. "I'm not mad at you. I'm just so afraid you'll hurt yourself again. Thank you for making breakfast, darling, but next time, let an adult do the cooking. If you're hungry, Marie will make your meals."

"I hear my name." Marie blew in through the back door into the kitchen with spots of paint on her cheek. "Ah, breakfast is ready. How nice of you, Frank!"

"Ruby made it." He arched an eyebrow.

"Oh? Then how very sweet of you, Ruby!" Unbothered by the situation, Marie walked around the table and seated herself.

"Marie, I don't want her cooking for us or waiting on us. She's a child."

"Alright, let it be as you wish, but she should have chores. Every child should have chores, don't you agree? That's how families run. I read all about it in *Good Housekeeping* magazine." Marie turned now to Ruby. "But since you have had a bad time with cooking in the past, let me or Frank do the cooking and baking. You can help me with the wash and keep your room clean. Is that fair?" Marie smiled and then motioned to Ruby to sit across from her.

"What about the dusting? I can do that." Ruby said as she slid into a chair.

"Dusting? Oh, I don't pay a lot of attention to that, although I should, I suppose." Marie waved her fork in the air. "It's just after years of house cleaning, I've discovered that dust returns within hours of wiping it away, so what's the use? It's a battle I certainly cannot win, and I'd never expect you to."

Frank and Marie burst out laughing. Ruby looked from Marie to Frank and then back again to Marie. "But I need to do more to earn my keep, ma'am. I need to keep on working, or—" Ruby felt this had to be settled. It would define her role in this household.

"Or what, Ruby?" Marie's bare foot with the red toenails began tapping against the floor. "Or we won't want you?"

It was out. She had guessed what Ruby was thinking. Marie not only expressed her feelings on canvas, but she just took Ruby's words right out of her mouth and placed them into the air where Ruby didn't know what to do with them. Lost in bewilderment and unintended opposition, Ruby opened and then shut her mouth, not knowing what to say next. If she said nothing, then perhaps they would speak for her again. This new couple confused her. Frank was jittery much of the time, while Marie seemed merry and relaxed down to her bones. In Ruby's old world, she knew how to act, but in this new one, it was baffling. What was wrong with these people?

"You don't have to work to earn your keep here, Ruby," Marie said, turning a bit crimson around the edges of her face. "Let's eat breakfast first. Then, we can go to town to shop. Would you like that, Ruby?"

Ruby looked up through the top of her eyelashes and nodded, hoping it was the proper response.

"Afterwards, we'll go to the hospital to see Andy. I can't wait to meet him!"

Ruby ate in jumpy silence and listened to Frank and Marie talk. Their conversation was filled with morsels of laughter between bites of food. However, Ruby feared they might be capable of changing house rules when she was least prepared. That concern made it hard to swallow her bacon. At long last, they left breakfast dishes soaking in sudsy water. Ruby shook her head; it ran against her grain to do that. The dishes needed to be cleaned and stacked inside the cupboards and the kitchen tidied.

Ruby climbed into the back of the truck while Marie and Frank sat together in the front. They drove to town, and Ruby memorized the landscape: route number to street names. As they turned onto McKinney Street, Ruby's heart sank when they passed the now vacant lot on Bell. People were hauling away scattered wood along with broken toys and scraps of forgotten laundry. Remnants of houses were discarded—life moved forward.

The truck wheeled around to Hickory Street and parked near the department store. Ruby would not have far to walk on her aching legs. When Marie opened her door and got out, no one paid any attention, but when Ruby tried to climb down from the back, people stopped to stare.

"Let me help you," Frank said. "Hold on to me."

"Mr. Frank," she said as politely as she knew. "I can manage myself. Thank you anyway for the careful handling of me in this condition."

"Pay no attention to stares. It's a small town," Marie whispered. "People enjoy their gossip.

Ruby was quite aware of every examining look that bore down on her and the whispers that circled them, passing from one mouth to another's ear. It was a nice change to finally be noticed, so she decided to be friendly and give a wave.

In Hanover's Department Store, Marie walked around the racks of clothes pushing through the dresses, smiling at some, and shaking her head at others. "What do you think, Ruby? Do you see anything here that looks good to you?"

"I don't know, ma'am." The large store was packed with everything imaginable. It was hard to concentrate on one thing. The shops in New York City she knew about specialized in food. She had never been inside of any other.

But here in Denton, they seemed to have it all in one place, making her wonder if there might be books nearby, too. She wanted to ask the man behind the counter, but with the odd smirk on his face, she decided not to speak.

"Well, I'm buying you a dress, so pick one." Marie studied the clothes.

"They all look beautiful to me."

"Take my advice: pick one quick before Frank has his say," Marie teased and then whispered, "He doesn't have good taste."

"Did I hear my name?" Frank peeked over the rack.

"Ruby is choosing a new dress."

"Wonderful, I want to help." Frank walked around to have a look.

"Brace yourself, Ruby."

"What about this one?" Frank held up a brown and black striped dress.

"Excuse me for saying, but I have spent a lot of time in that color, so it might be good to try something new."

"Okay, no brown or black dresses."

Marie pulled out a blue print dress that buttoned down the back. It was trimmed with lace. "How does this one appeal to your senses?"

Ruby's hands flew to her mouth, and she nodded her head excitedly. "It's the prettiest dress I have ever seen."

"Good. I think it's pretty, too, just like you." Marie spoke in a genuine way that let Ruby know this was easy but no big deal to Marie—only it was a huge deal to Ruby. She wanted to show Marie her appreciation, so she kept on talking.

"Nobody's ever gotten me anything like this in my whole life. I'll take good care of it, too, just wait and see." Ruby studied every white pearl button down the back. She ran her hand lightly over the fabric, stopping at the curved waistline, pleased she'd have a shape and not be one thin, long line anymore from her shoulders down to the bottom hem. Ruby noticed Marie's face filling with joy right along with hers, as though she may have suddenly realized what a treat this was.

"That is the biggest smile I've seen on you yet, Miss Ruby Red. I'm glad we were able to put it there. Go ahead into the changing room and try it on right now," Marie suggested.

"Changing room?" Ruby wobbled about while trying to figure out what that might be.

"Excuse me," Mr. Hanover said, stepping into the conversation, "Did I hear you tell her to try on the clothes?"

"Yes, I did," Marie said with a lift of her head. "Ruby, right there. See those curtains? That is the changing room. Take off the clothes you have on, and put this dress on to make sure it fits, while Mr. Hanover and I have a little talk. Be sure to pull the curtain all the way closed. We'll be waiting right here for you."

Ruby took the hanger from Marie. She held it high in the air to keep the dress hem from dragging on the wood floor, never taking her eyes from it, not for a second. Ruby was in a little piece of Heaven when she slipped on the dress and walked proudly out to show everyone.

"It fits me just fine."

Marie selected a few more dresses in shades of yellow and pink, despite all the heavy sighs Mr. Hanover was heaving.

Ruby stopped her. "Mrs. Marie, you need only buy me this one dress. I can wash it out each night before bed and sleep with my fingers crossed that it will be dry enough to wear by daylight."

"How many days are in a week? Marie asked.

"Seven, ma'am."

Marie counted out six dresses, a jacket, two sweaters, underclothes, two nightgowns, and then lightweight knee socks. She said, "These should cover your legs to keep meddlesome people from staring."

"I really must step in, Mrs. Bindle," Mr. Hanover interrupted again, a sour look on his face. "I hope you plan on buying everything she tries on because there is no way my white customers will buy any of it now, and I will be out a pile of money."

"Of course we are buying it all," Frank said.

"And there will be no returns."

"No returns," Marie agreed.

Ruby stood at the counter, watching her pile of clothes grow taller and taller. She pinched herself because she believed that this moment couldn't be real. In her most imaginative moment, she might have hoped to go into a store and come out with one dress. She kept on smiling until her jaws ached again, but couldn't make herself stop because of it. The elation was just too great to hold back.

Next to her pile of clothes was a second pile of clothes meant for Andy. And then, Frank added a stuffed tiger right on top. "Is there anything special you'd like, Ruby?'

"If I were given one more wish, it would be a book."

"Do you have any books here?" Frank asked the store clerk.

"Right back corner of the store."

Ruby walked to a shelf that held ten books. She ran her fingers across the spines and smelled the pages. After careful consideration, she held out her choice.

"The Voyages of Doctor Dolittle, by Hugh Lofting. Seems like a good choice," Frank said.

Just when Ruby thought everything had been purchased, then came the biggest surprise of the morning. Frank asked the store clerk to measure Ruby for a special pair of built-up shoes. "One of her legs is shorter than the other, and I want her to walk easily," Frank told Mr. Hanover, a small man stooped over at the shoulders.

"Oh, Mr. Frank, will I walk even again? It won't hurt so badly anymore?"

"Yes, Ruby, you can walk 'even' again. And with a bit of luck, the pain should decrease."

"Thanks, Mr. Frank, Mrs. Marie."

"Let me get my tape measure to see what size she wears and how high the sole should be built up," Mr. Hanover said in a business-like tone.

While she waited for him to locate his measurement tool, Ruby leaned on the counter where she saw the store bell and tapped it. Bing, bing, bing.

"Sit in that chair." Mr. Hanover pointed. Once seated, Ruby extended her feet, and the clerk pulled his spectacles from the top of his forehead down over his eyes. Each time he took a size reading, he wrote it down. With the order finished, he said the shoes would arrive in a few weeks.

"Can't have your cleaning girl limping about the house," Mr. Hanover said in good humor. "Here, take this cane for her. It's on me. You keep her strong and well, and you'll get lots of good years out of this young one."

"I certainly appreciate your advice." Marie politely accepted the cane and winked at Ruby as though they were conspirators. "But Miss Ruby Red will not be cleaning any more than any other white child in town."

"Oh?"

Following Marie's example, Ruby also thanked Mr. Hanover for the cane and accepted it from Marie.

Frank hooked his arm around Marie's waist and walked her toward the door. "Come, Ruby."

22

Andy slept beneath white starched hospital sheets. Marie and Frank waited in the doorway, allowing Ruby to enter the room first. Andy turned toward the sound of footsteps. His face was covered in cuts and bruises ripe with hues of blue and green and yellow. A large knot the size of a baseball sat in the middle of his forehead. Andy brightened when he saw her. "Ruby! You're here!"

"I kept my promise." She grabbed his hand.

"You did. I'm sorry I said I hated you. I didn't really mean it."

"I know you didn't." Ruby turned toward the doorway and spilled her thoughts as a gushing, babbling brook. "Andy, this is Mr. Frank and his—Mrs. Marie. They said we could live in their house, and your room is right across from mine. It's the truth. I saw it with my own eyes. There are pictures of sail boats on the walls, and there's a tree outside your window with a bird's nest on a branch."

Andy's eyes teared. "Really, Ruby? We'll be together?"

Marie snatched the tiger from Frank. She plopped it on Andy's lap. "I hope you like tigers."

Andy wrapped his arms around it and hugged hard. "Tigers are fine, but I have to know if there are bears at your house. I don't like bears."

"No bears, not even a real tiger," Frank said, now standing over the bed.

Marie brushed back Andy's hair with her fingers.

"It sounds great then." Andy's eyes started to close.

"Come on now, ladies. Let's leave. Andy needs his rest."

Andy's eyes shot open. "No, don't go."

"The doctor said we could only stay for a short moment this time," Frank said, walking toward the door. "Rest, Andy, so you can come home soon."

"Ruby, don't leave me here alone. It's so scary." He swallowed hard. "Take me with you now."

Ruby turned to Frank.

"We'll come to see you every day."

"But I want to go now!" Andy pleaded. "I'll die here!"

"It'll be all right." Ruby tried to soothe him. She looked out the window. "Hey, I can see the train tracks outside. Can you hear the train's whistle when it goes by?"

Andy blinked back tears and nodded his head. "I think so."

"When you hear the train, think of me, and I will be thinking of you, and then you won't feel alone. And soon, we'll be back in Mr. Frank's truck to bring you home forever."

"Don't forget about me, Ruby."

"Andy, I could never forget you. I love you."

23
.....
Days Later

The radio was at full volume. The singer sounded as if his lungs were bursting when he belted out, "Someone's in the kitchen with Din-ah!" Marie sang right along while she kneaded bread dough.

"Someone's in the kitchen I kno-o-ow. Someone's in the kitchen with Dinah—strumming on the old banjo!"

"Great weather for baking bread!" she said, slamming her fists into the dough and flipping her hair back with a turn of her head. "Ruby, how old are you? When is your birthday? I want to mark it on the calendar." She nodded her head toward the wall where the page was flipped open to July 15, 1921.

"Oh, I'm not real sure of my age. Mama Burke told me that I was about five when they found me on the street. I stayed with them for six years before I was told to leave." She relayed the pieces of information matter-of-factly.

"Told to leave? Who told you to leave?" Marie's voice was sharp, as though she wanted to find and scold whoever did such a thing.

"Mrs. Stone was the lady of the mansion. I was her servant—one of her servants. Mama and Papa Burke lived there, too. But they weren't my parents. I just called them that. I don't like thinking about her or the day she sent me away. Although her sending me away in the snow eventually led me here where I am much happier."

"Why did she send you away?" Marie stopped working with the dough and looked at Ruby as if it were the most important question she had ever asked.

"Oh, boy, did I ever do something really bad," Ruby answered bluntly and held her gaze.

"And what would that be?"

"I picked up a doll that was meant for Miss Betsy's Christmas present. I had no right to do it. It was my entire fault. And because of me, Papa Burke died." The end of her nose tingled, and tears flooded her eyes. "He died because I was bad."

"What? Surely, you have caused no one's death."

"In here, I know what you're saying is true." Ruby pointed at her head. Then she laid her hand on her chest. "But, in here, I know I did cause it."

"Well, if the cause of Mr. Burke was due to you holding a doll, he would be the first one to die of such a thing, and I assure you, there is no medical term for it. Little girls will act like little girls, especially when there is a doll involved."

Ruby had held back each time she had wanted to touch Frank or Marie. She felt nervous about touching white people. But now, the matter was taken out of her hands when Marie put her arms around Ruby and hugged her to her bosom and held her there. It caused a slight panic to Ruby because she couldn't breathe well with her nose pressed into Marie. Knowing she was reaching the end of her oxygen, a thousand thoughts ran through her head in that one instant. What if Marie kept on hugging her? Ruby could tell by the look on Marie's face that she thought it was a very sad story and felt her hug must be comforting. Perhaps Ruby shouldn't have put so much emotion into her experience because these passions now rose up in Marie—and she may not be able to shake them off anytime soon. For the sake of not suffocating, would it be impolite to pull away? It might just make Marie think she wasn't appreciative of the hug.

Just as Ruby thought she was drawing near to death, Mrs. Marie stepped backwards. "Girls are attracted to dolls. It was only natural for you to want to hold one. And for that, you were tossed out. There is nothing wrong with acting on your natural impulse. Have you ever had a doll of your own?"

"Why, yes, I had a doll! It was a good one, too. Mama Burke made me one." Ruby huffed out her words.

"She made you one? I bet it was pretty. Come with me." Marie wiped her hands on a wet cloth and left the kitchen.

As they passed through the parlor, Ruby noticed Marie's most recent painting had prairie flowers tinged with brown along the edges while all the others were in full bloom and filled with color.

"I have a question, Mrs. Marie."

"Ask."

"How come you live way out here and not in town?"

"Because—it's hard to explain. But to put it simply, I don't really care for most people. I like my solitude. I also like what I see in the country much more than what is in town. Bricks and mortar hold no charm. I like wind and rain and flowers."

"I like wind and rain and flowers, too!"

Marie stopped in front of the hall closet. She opened the door and drug out an old humpback trunk decorated in tin. "This trunk came all the way from Italy many years ago."

An immediate musty odor surged into the air, causing Ruby to rear back on her heels. After a few minutes, the air cleared. The top tray exposed a bevy of items that clearly had not seen daylight for a number of years, so perfect they remained: loose pictures, a scrapbook, bundles of letters tied with ribbon, a shawl, a baby sweater, a jumble of old hats. Marie removed the tray and set it on the floor, then reached so far down into the trunk that her head nearly disappeared from sight. Finally, she sat back on her heels and smiled. In her arms, she held a porcelain doll with coal black hair and brown eyes that opened and then clunked closed. "Mama!" the doll moaned. The mohair wasn't smooth like the Christmas doll; it stuck out in all directions. The dress was wrinkled and stained with age.

Marie's eyes smiled. "This is my doll. She was a gift to me on my eighth birthday. I'm sure it's not as special as the one Mrs. Burke made, but I want you to have it."

"Oh, no!" Ruby put her hands behind her back, afraid to touch the doll.

Marie lowered the doll into her lap and thought a bit. Suddenly, she seemed to remember something. "Guess what? Today is the 15th of July. I am breaking the news to you that today is your birthday!"

"It is?" Ruby leaned forward with great interest. "How do you know?"

"From time to time, things come to me inside of my head. A voice tells me. And I heard that voice tell me right this instant that today is the day of your birth."

"Are you sure that's what it said?"

"Sure as we are sitting here, it whispered, 'today is Ruby's birthday.'"

Ruby shivered with excitement.

"Since you aren't sure of how old you are, how old would you like to be?"

"Didn't your voice mention how old I am?" Ruby asked.

"No. No mention. So you get to decide. If I were to advise you, I would say a low number rather than a high number. Tell me."

"I don't know. I've never thought about it."

"Well, think about it now. How old would you like to be?"

"I would like to be twelve." Ruby couldn't help but laugh. Mrs. Marie's silliness was contagious.

"Then it shall be. And this doll is your present, so you must take it. It is now your doll forever. I will never take it back. Let's go bake a cake. We shall eat it after dinner for dessert. Or maybe we will eat it before dinner! We could switch up dinner and dessert. Dinner could be the cake and dessert can be whatever we would normally have for dinner! We'll even save a piece to bring to Andy. It's your birthday, and we will do anything you'd like. Do you prefer chocolate or white cake?" Marie talked so fast that it was hard to keep up with her.

"I've never had a cake of my own before." Ruby felt as confused as if she had been hit in the head with another piece of wood.

"Then we shall make two cakes, a white cake and a chocolate cake, and you shall have them both!" Marie put the trunk away and hurried back to the kitchen.

Ruby sat on the hallway floor for a long time looking at the doll that once belonged to Marie and now belonged to her. The hair had been cut down to the scalp in some places; there were small chips along the nose and hairline. Ruby loved it more than she could have ever loved the Christmas doll.

At dinner, Ruby decided her favorite cake was the white cake *and* the chocolate cake. That made Marie laugh uproariously, while Frank looked on with a thin, worried smile. Ruby wondered where the worry came from.

When day turned to night, Ruby lay in her iron bed, covered by a quilt next to Marie's well-loved doll. A train rumbled in the distance, and the whistle blew—maybe Andy heard it, too. On her way to sleep, Ruby thought about Andy sleeping in the hospital bed. She imagined Mama Burke looking up at the stars when she carried out the day's trash and swept the sidewalks from house to street, wondering what became of that little girl she loved so much. If Papa Burke had gotten tired of being a ghost in the grand house, perhaps he was dancing on streets made of gold. She was sure Myna knelt by her bed and talked to God as though talking to a friend. And then she thought of her mother still in her red coat, calling Ruby's name.

"I'm right here, Mother. Safe."

24
.....

Ruby sensed a shift in herself.

The hospital visits ran together in a wonderful blur of talking, laughing, and hugs. The routine of seeing Andy almost every morning became blissfully uneventful that she couldn't remember day to day what they talked about. She even allowed herself to think about the future now. Her fear of making mistakes dulled. It was comforting to discover that Marie and Frank were white folk who not only kept their word, but also took her to see Andy. This grew seeds of trust inside of her like a sprout reaching for the warm sun. As a thank you, she included them in her goodnight prayers right beside all the rest of people she loved—which didn't include Mrs. Stone or Miss Betsy. Even though they were the ones most in need of prayer, she just couldn't bring herself to wish any goodness upon them.

Today was Sunday. A special day Sunday.

"Now that you've settled in, it's time to show you off at church. Let them know you are a part of this family. Today, you will see black families up in the balcony. But you won't sit there. You will sit with us and the other white families on the main floor." Mrs. Marie hammered the silverware down on the table.

Ruby wasn't altogether sure what that meant. All she cared about was Frank fixing breakfast. He cracked open brown eggs, sending their gooey contents into the hot, black pan. Thick slabs of hickory-smoked bacon sizzled in another other pan. He served fat, doughy pancakes topped with butter, maple syrup, and berries.

"Are you sure that's a good idea, Marie? Taking Ruby to church? We can leave her here while we go. You wouldn't mind, would you, Ruby?'

Ruby shook her head.

Marie looked at Frank like a fly that needed to be swatted. "Nonsense. You of all people would know with that paper of yours. Times are changing."

"Well, they aren't changing fast enough, especially around here. I hated for Ruby to see the move from Quakertown. Do you know the woman's committee told me that the monies raised for the new park also included a new fair grounds?"

"And it's not included," Marie simply stated.

"But I printed it just the same because that is what I was told by the Denton Women's Club. That alone could have swayed public opinion on Quakertown's demise."

Ruby struggled to understand this adult business that Mr. Frank said he didn't quite understand himself. To her, it was all mixed in with who had the final say and how much people liked the person who had the final say in things, which usually settled the matter altogether.

"Hush and pass the pancakes. Syrup, too. Don't forget the butter." Marie smiled at Ruby and then placed two on her plate, smearing them with butter. "No sense in getting a jumbled stomach mixed in with breakfast."

"These are the best I ever made. Don't you agree, Marie? Ruby?" Frank asked with his mouth filled.

"Mind your manners now, Frank. We have a young lady living in our home now and must be proper examples." Marie took a bite. "Yes, they are only a *little* doughy this time."

"You're getting better, Mr. Frank!"

Breakfast devoured, they dumped all the dishes into the sudsy sink and dressed for church. Ruby loved every single one of her new dresses. Sometimes, it was hard to choose which to wear. Ruby scratched her head in careful consideration and picked the yellow dress with a bow in front.

She stared at herself in the mirror, amazed how comfortable she felt living this new life. It was as though she always belonged. Change was easy when you saw it coming like with Mrs. Stone. But when happiness walked away in the form of her mother, it was unexpected and left pain that still ached.

Would living with the Bindles be different? Only time would reveal it to her. Marie did have a voice whisper in her ear from time to time. It could be a worrisome voice should it turn against Ruby.

The moment Ruby settled in between Frank and Marie on the wooden pew in the middle of the church, white folks, already seated nearby, gathered their belongings and moved to the already full benches. To Ruby, the murmurs sounded a lot like hens cackling.

"Are they mad at us?" Ruby whispered to Marie.

"Nothing to be mad about." Marie opened her Bible. "Pay them no mind."

Ruby glanced around at the pouty faces.

"Should we sit up there in the balcony?"

"They wouldn't like Frank and me up there any more than others like you down here. And you're staying with us. Now, we need to be quiet so we can hear the preacher say his piece."

Ruby sucked in a deep breath and raised her eyes, hoping there wouldn't be church trouble on her account.

The minister, Reverend Willie Clark had a deep, echoing voice. She bet everyone at the train station three miles away could hear him. Sitting atop his tapered nose were eyeglasses. He smiled a whole lot, as if he had just finished talking matters over with the Lord and liked what He had to say. Church felt right. It was a good way to start each week.

Ruby looked up at the stained glass windows with the sunshine flooding through them. Their brilliant colors covered her. She felt safe despite the trouble earlier.

Reverend Clark interrupted her thoughts. "We have new worshipers with us this morning I want you to meet. The Bindles—who by the way, we have missed you for the last few Sundays—have taken in a girl by the name of Ruby Red. Ruby, we welcome you to our town, our community, our church, and into our hearts."

Midst the weak applause, Ruby slowly nodded. Not

able to talk at such a solemn moment of greeting, she sat back down.

"I have another introduction to make. We have been keeping a secret ourselves," the Reverend continued cheerfully. "My wife, Bertha, and I have longed for a family. By way of adoption, we had planned on giving a younger child, preferably a baby, a place in our family when the Orphan Train came through. However, God had someone else for us. No one was as surprised as us when the baby turned out to be half grown. I know what y'all must be thinking."

Chuckling and squeaking pews resonated through the arched ceiling.

"Since my wife and I are barely into our twenties, how can we manage someone about to enter their teens? Well, he needed a home. And we needed a son. I felt God speaking to us to take on this parentless child and bring him up in the way of the Lord. After weeks of prayer, patience, and coaxing, he finally agreed to come to church with us today."

"Amen," several members shouted.

"Louie, would you please stand? This is our son. He comes to us from New York City by way of the Orphan Train. Same as Ruby."

Mrs. Clark and Louie sat on the front row and turned to face the congregation to receive a rousing applause. When Ruby caught sight of Louie's ugly face, she knew there was trouble smiling back at her. The young reverend had taken in a lunatic.

The parishioners stood and clapped again to greet the two new children.

After church, Ruby climbed into Frank's truck and didn't think this day could get any worse than seeing Louie, but then she saw the Stickman who had beaten her and Andy. There he was, driving down the street in his raggedy old truck as if he hadn't done a single thing wrong in his entire life. A sickness of hatred filled her innards. She wanted to call Frank's attention to him but figured she'd keep her peace for now because she was still figuring out how things worked around here. It was best to be careful and sneaky about it and save this deed for another day. Even knowing that she might be sent away for doing something sneaky, being sneaky always interested Ruby.

25

After church, just past noon, a handsome black couple unexpectedly called on the Bindles.

Ford and Elda Crawford brought their two boys who unabashedly hung from tree branches and did cart wheels in the yard while Ruby remained on the steps near the adults. She had never been comfortable with those her age.

Ruby helped Marie line the porch railings with plates of heart-shaped sugar cookies and handed tall glasses of lemonade to everyone. Marie appeared relaxed, rocking back and forth in the chair, dark tendrils of hair floating about her head in the warm afternoon breeze. It was obvious to Ruby that Frank was glad for the company because of his friendly chatter and wide toothy grins.

"It'd be nice for Ruby to have friends like Joel and James," he said. "Come by any time."

Ruby snapped her head around in disbelief and nearly choked on her drink.

"Would you enjoy that, Ruby?" Marie asked sweetly with a lift of her brow.

"Yes, ma'am." Ruby skirted the truth and went back to nibbling on her cookie. No way did she ever want to play with those rough boys.

"I hope you don't mind us stopping by like this, but we took a family outing after church, and decided to come meet Ruby. And say 'hello' to you as well, of course." Mrs. Crawford smoothed her dress over her knees.

"Very thoughtful of you." Frank leaned in the doorway.

"We now live out on Solomon Hill." Mrs. Crawford focused her eyes on Ruby.

"We'd hoped you would remain in town." Frank frowned.

"Are you settled in?" Marie asked.

"As much as can be expected, but I'm not happy about it. No one is. Work is in town, and we were pushed miles into the country. We had to buy this wagon and horse just to get to Ford's grocery store."

"No complaining please, Elda." Mr. Crawford patted her hand.

"Evidently the city felt a park was much preferred down the hill from the university than our homes were to us." Sadness clouded the woman's face. "Heaven save those white college girls from having to cast their eyes upon the black folk of this community. We are good enough to take on the jobs no one else wants like laundering and gardening and cleaning, but we aren't good enough to live so close to them."

"Elda!" Mr. Crawford's voice was harsh.

Ruby's chest tightened with sorrow, remembering the sight of the black folk being forced from their homes. That first day greeting was one she'd never forget. It was a harsh reminder of how one could be safe in bed one night and wandering the streets the very next. It happened to her. It happened to others. Ruby knew she shouldn't join adult conversations, but she didn't stop herself this time. "Why not put the park someplace else?"

Fanning herself, Mrs. Crawford smiled broadly at Ruby. "Exactly!"

"It's quite complex," Frank said. "You see, Ruby, the College of Industrial Arts is directly up the hill from Quakertown. It's a women's college, and some were concerned with the safety of young women attending college there so close to—" Frank cut himself off, unsure how to finish his thought.

"What he isn't saying, child, is that the college wanted to enlarge their liberal arts program," Mrs. Crawford said.

"What's that?"

"Art, music, literature." Marie smiled.

"The stipulation was that the white women who attend the college needed to be shielded from the black part of town. It's true. They didn't want to walk through muddy streets. Fix them for the white folk but not for the black. We hang laundry in our yards, and they called it 'unsightly.' And they didn't like our children playing out in the street. Scoot them away! Scoot them all away! By the way, I noticed the Bindles' names weren't among the signatures on the petition, thank you for that," Mrs. Crawford added.

"I would never sign such a heinous piece of paper." Marie adamantly shook her head. "Just this morning, Frank and I discussed how they even tricked the Denton Record Newspaper by saying that they needed the land for a park *and* a fair grounds when only the park will be built."

"I don't care what they wanted to use Quakertown for, it shouldn't have been for sale." Now Frank was angry.

"They just came and took it from you then?" Ruby looked to Mrs. Crawford, hoping that wasn't right.

"Amen, Brother Bindle, and yes, Ruby." Mrs. Crawford demurely pressed a hankie to her lips.

"It's Sunday. I think the Lord would have us discuss other matters." Mr. Crawford shuffled his feet uncomfortably. "You can imagine how surprising it was to see you with this young girl in church in the main section and not up in the balcony."

"Oh?" Marie acted as if she had no idea what he was getting at.

"Yes," Mrs. Crawford said, "Ruby seems like such a darling girl, on the verge on being a young woman. We were wondering about her people."

"Not sure of her people," Frank answered. "It seems she hopped the Orphan Train."

"I remember you writing about that train a few years ago," Mr. Crawford said.

"We are blessed to have her with us." Marie sipped her drink and rocked her chair a little quicker.

"Gossip is she's your servant girl." Mr. Crawford said, easing his way into the reason for the visit. His hair was cropped close to his scalp.

Wondering why they were so curious about her, Ruby leaned forward to hear every word but pretended to be distracted with a bee buzzing around her drink.

"Do you always listen to gossip? How sad for you." The corners of Marie's mouth turned down before she snapped up to her feet. Frank gave his wife a look that said to hold her temper. Marie heeded the glare and sat back down.

"Next time, please tell them that Marie and I are her guardians," Frank explained. "We do not employ servants."

Frank's words liberated Ruby who felt that perhaps things would turn out alright for her after all.

"I don't mean to be disrespectful, but don't you think Ruby would be more comfortable living with someone more like her?" Mrs. Crawford asked.

"She is living with someone like her. We're both girls," Marie said, grinning mischievously.

A surprise giggle burst from Ruby's lips, but she quickly covered her mouth.

After a few more carefully measured words of polite courtesy, the Crawfords stood, indicating they were ready to leave. Mr. Crawford walked to the edge of the step and said, "Mr. and Mrs. Bindle, we certainly did not mean to offend you in any measure, so please forgive us if we have done so. You must know that having this girl live with you is quite unheard of and unusual. We aren't the only ones in town who feel she needs to be with her kind on Solomon Hill. Think of how Quakertown was razed in just a few months. Repercussions still reverberate through this community. Should this not work out for you for any reason, we would be happy to have Ruby come live with us."

Ruby noticed the sudden wash of tears in Marie's eyes.

"You see, my twin boys busted out my womb when they were born, and I can't have anymore children," Mrs. Crawford said with tears also filling her eyes. "I so prayed for a girl."

"Elda, stop," Mr. Crawford pleaded.

"No, I have to say this—when we saw Ruby sitting in church alongside of you, I thought my prayers for a daughter had been answered."

"I am truly sorry about your situation," Marie said softening. "Quakertown or Solomon Hill, Ruby is not a piece of land that can or will be taken away; she is a person with a heart and a soul and a mind of her own. Her home is here with Frank and me."

Now Ruby knew. Marie not only saw the outside of her but the inside as well. Ruby gave her the biggest smile of her life.

Mrs. Crawford pulled Marie to the side of the porch and whispered, "There's something else you should consider."

"Oh?" Marie raised her eyebrows.

"I heard talk that you—" She wrung her hands.

"Quiet, Elda!" her husband blurted. "We can all hear you. This isn't the time or the place."

"Ruby, go play in the yard," Frank said.

Ruby didn't move. Her heart beat quicker, and her hands prickled with nerves.

"It's still something that needs to be said. Mrs. Bindle, I heard talk that you aren't always feeling well. That you have—spells that you refer to as 'voices.' Surely, that is not good for a child to be around."

"I'm a young lady," Ruby murmured beneath her breath, but no one seemed to be paying attention to her now. Ruby furrowed her brow and looked at Marie. So far, the voices hadn't caused any problems.

Marie look down, noticed her bewilderment, and took Ruby's hand. She stared Mrs. Crawford down defiantly.

"Alright, I shall regard it as gossip then." Mrs. Crawford turned to the young girl, "Goodbye, Ruby, dear. You are a lovely young lady, and we're most delighted to have met you. If you ever get a mind to and it's alright with the Bindles, please come to our home for a visit. I am sure Joel and James would enjoy that."

"Yes, ma'am," Ruby answered, though she never ever wanted to see any of them ever again after the way they upset Marie.

26

August 1, 1921

Andy was coming home!

This was the first day Ruby felt fully happy in her entire life. "Home" was a comforting word. On this perfect day of utter happiness, Ruby noticed nurses huddled in tight circles talking quietly. Some cried. A doctor asked to speak to Frank and Marie alone, so Ruby was sent to sit on a chair with a magazine. She picked up one called Farm News with a picture of a pig on the front. Ruby pretended to read but kept her eyes on her new family talking to the doctor. Just like the nurses, Marie began to cry and slumped against Frank who wiped his face with the backs of his hands before putting them around his wife.

Finally, they looked back at Ruby. Grief veiled their faces. She swallowed hard. The magazine slid down her legs and fell onto the clean, waxed floor. In slow motion, Frank walked over to her and knelt, his large white hands folding over her small black ones. His voice faltered as he explained what happened: "Andy crossed to the other side early this morning. There was a blood clot in his brain. They worked hard to save him, but there was no saving him. He wasn't in any pain."

Ruby shifted her eyes. To know Andy passed without pain didn't make his passing any easier. Tears pooled at the corners of her eyes. Her arms and legs went numb. There were no thoughts left in her head. Did Marie's voices have something to say about it?

They drove back home in silence.

Ruby charged through the front door and bumped into the walls trying to get up the steps and into her room, blinded by her own tears. The door to her room slammed behind her, and she kicked it before falling face forward onto her bed where she beat the pillow until feathers floated about the room. Even spilling the hot grease from the cook pot onto her legs didn't hurt near as fierce as this, and she had nearly died from that pain. Her chest hurt. Her lungs felt raw when she tried to take deep breaths. Hot tears fell from her eyes and soaked her sheets. Her world, which now held beauty, plunged back into darkness.

Wanting to see Andy's room, she left her bed and opened the door to the room with the sailboat wallpaper. The tiger sat middle of the bed, but Andy would never sleep there. She and Andy would never watch the bird's nest together from his window. There'd be no late-night utterings back and forth across the hallway. She would never hear his little voice again. Would never again she set eyes on his freckles. Screaming with realization, Ruby returned to her bed. Marie stood at the door and begged Ruby to stop, but Ruby refused to be consoled or touched.

By midnight, Ruby had worn herself completely out. Marie tiptoed into the room. This time, Ruby allowed

Marie to hold her. She felt Marie's heart beating as Marie held her and rocked her back and forth into the wee hours of the morning.

They had to plan a funeral for Andy—a little freckled-faced boy who had never spent one night beneath their roof, but he had still been family. Reverend Clark was particularly solemn as he spoke over Andy's small coffin. Sitting near his new mother, Louie looked genuinely upset. The rims of his eyes were red. Ruby wondered if it was from crying or something else, but he seemed to be properly grieving. Ruby thought about the terrible battle he and Andy had gotten in to the day by the stream. Rub wondered what caused the change in him now. How she wished she could switch Louie with Andy. In her anguish, she refused to be charitable.

Reverend Clark spoke from his pulpit.

"Marie, Frank, Ruby—I see the pain you are suffering. Grieving is a sign of having loved someone. Andy came to this town as a homeless, fatherless, motherless waif. He found family here in Denton along with Louie and Ruby. Today, I look out, and I see his mother and his father, his sister and his friends. Keep a special memory of him with you for the rest of your life, and he will always be part of who you are. Andy will not only live forever in Heaven, but also on this earth as long as your feet walk it. Make your life count for Andy."

As they walked to the cemetery, Ruby pulled on Marie's arm. "Why him? Why not Louie who acts like he's good when he's really not? Why not someone like Mrs. Stone back in New York? She makes everyone miserable, so what good is she? Why not Stickman who beat Andy? Why not—someone like me?"

"Ruby." Frank stopped walking and turned to her. "Things happen in life that we cannot explain."

Ruby wiped her tears on her dress sleeve. "I need to know, Mr. Frank. Was Andy too small and beautiful and perfect to live longer on this earth with all its trouble? His journey to finding a home had taken him so far—perhaps he burned himself up in a small lifetime where it takes some of us years to do that."

"His light went to the stars. Ruby, we have suffered a great loss in not knowing Andy like you did. I want you to tell us about him every day so we can know him, too. I believe his earthly light is now a star," Marie said.

"Mrs. Marie, I'm not sure that will help, but I will think that, too."

The other people from church cried as if Andy had been a special part of their lives all his life. They had not even laid eyes on him until that moment in the open casket with his arms crossed upon his chest. Even in death, his red hair refused to lie flat. Ruby thought he looked so peaceful, like he did all those nights they had slept close together on the train, riding their dreams to Texas. When she'd gone up to the casket, it was hard not to shake him, not to tell him to get up and come home with her to the blue sailboat room across the hall from her room. She wanted Marie to give him a birthday with a party like the one she had been given. Maybe there would be a present inside that trunk for Andy, too.

"What is your favorite cake, white or chocolate? We

will make them both," Marie would have told him. And then Andy would have declared that they both were his favorite, just like Ruby.

But now, the lid had closed, and the coffin had been lowered into the ground.

There would be no birthday for Andy, no present from the trunk, no cake. The best anyone could do for him now was what had been done already: new clothes for the coffin, gentle words spoken about a gentle child, and kind people who came to church to cry and mourn his passing with his family.

Days later, Ruby and Marie returned to the cemetery with a wagon bursting with prairie flowers for his grave.

"I will make sure a garden always grows here." Ruby began to dig the ground and spoke to Andy's headstone, "Find Papa Burke, and tell him we're family. I'm certain he must be tired of hanging around Mrs. Stone's house by now and has fluttered off to his great reward. Papa Burke will take good care of you."

By the time they had finished, there were a half dozen butterflies enjoying their flowers.

The following morning, the sun anointed her room, and a cool breeze swept through the open window. Something touched her face, causing Ruby to stir. It felt like the corner of a curtain slowly moving across her cheeks and nose. She opened her eyes to see a butterfly fluttering about her face. When she sat up, it flew to the foot of the iron bed. She crawled to the end of the bed, and it flew to the windowsill. Ruby slipped out of bed and went to the window. This elegant insect wasn't lost like other bugs that fly into the house and can't figure how to leave. This one entered and exited gracefully and intentionally. Ruby stood at the window. The garden below was alive with what seemed to be every kind of Texas butterfly. Not even Marie with all her talented imagination could have captured this magical moment on canvas.

27

Days later, Frank left for work. He was covering a trial in rural East Texas for the Denton Record, leaving Ruby and Marie alone with each other. As always, Marie accepted his trips—requiring long periods away from home, many times without contact—but it was hard for Ruby.

Ruby was up by eight. She came downstairs fully dressed, marveling at how easy it was to sleep this late, while feeling guilty about it, wondering if the ways of her former life would ever completely wear away.

She passed through the living room and noticed furniture skewed in odd directions. "Mrs. Marie, what's going on with the davenport?" As Ruby entered the kitchen, she stopped dead in her tracks.

"Hi, cutie!" Marie greeted Ruby with a kiss on her cheek.

Ruby touched the fleeting peck on her check and noticed a paintbrush tucked behind Marie's ear. She wore a paint-spattered apron over her nightgown.

"About time you got up."

"How long have you been up?" Ruby asked, looking around the disordered room.

"Actually, I haven't been to bed yet. There are so many ideas dancing around inside of my head. I can't seem to get them all down on canvas fast enough. Look. Tell me what you think."

Ruby slowly turned around to see painted canvases drying on chair rails. "Mrs. Marie, there must be five new paintings."

"Seven. Two more outside on the porch. The sky is this amazing color when it creeps over the horizon. It's so hard to capture the exact color, and then just when I think I have, it changes into something even more exquisite." She chattered away enthusiastically. "In this painting, we see dropped petals of Mexican hat and Indian mallow. Look at the bluebonnets in this one!"

"Mrs. Marie, I find it rather sad that all the flowers are dying in these pictures. Why?"

Marie didn't answer; she busied herself by packing a box with paintbrushes, water, turpentine, tubes of paint colors, canvas, a sketchpad, and empty bottles whose outsides were smeared with dried paint. "Let's hurry. If you're hungry, grab bread and toast it. I just have to pack our sandwiches and pour lemonade into glass jars, and we'll be all set to go as soon as I change."

"Go where?" Ruby asked. Marie could be dizzying.

"Didn't I tell you last night?" Marie seemed muddled as she pulled on a lock of her hair.

Ruby shook her head.

"The voices—sometimes things get jumbled up in my head." She laughed. "Today, right this very minute, we are going in search of inspiration for something we both can paint!"

"Like what?" Ruby asked, setting bread into the metal toaster over the stove burners.

"We shall know what to paint when we see it! We will discover it along the way. But the important thing is to keep our minds busy. I saw a doctor once about my voices. He said to keep busy. So I am. Busy as a bee. Where is your hairbrush?" Marie left the room and shortly returned with it.

"A good mother brushes her daughter's hair." Marie held up the brush, not sure where to start.

"I can do it myself if you'd like."

"Let me try." Marie started at the scalp and pulled the bristles back but tangled the brush in Ruby's curly hair. "Did that hurt?"

"It did."

"Let me try again." But the results were the same. "Never mind. We can fuss with your hair later. In the meantime, I picked these buttercups from the yard just before you got up. I thought how pretty they would look in your hair."

"You're putting all those flowers in my hair?" Ruby smiled, delighted there were so many.

"Yes, all of them." Marie tucked them here and there, securing them with bobby pins, until Ruby's head looked like a garden.

When she finished, they put Marie's paint supplies along with the picnic lunch in the wagon. Pulling it around the corner of the house, they bumped into Mrs. Crawford.

"You two look like you are in a hurry to get somewhere." Mrs. Crawford eyed Ruby's hair critically. She held up a small brown paper sack.

"We are in search of a picture to paint!" Ruby announced, trying to match her displeasure with Marie's at uninvited company.

"And having a picnic lunch along the way," Marie added.

"I won't keep you then," Mrs. Crawford spoke uncomfortably. "I'll leave this sack with you. Inside is an herbal ointment for treating Ruby's scarred legs. I also brought some special oil for her hair. Makes it nice and shiny to keep it from getting all dried out like it is now. Things white folk don't know about."

"Thank you, ma'am." Ruby softened, taking the sack.

"I would like to be in Ruby's life, if you don't mind." Mrs. Crawford pursed her lips slightly.

"I hope Ruby's new life here will encompass many friends. I know we both will regard you as one of them," Marie said. She pulled the wagon, heading down the road.

Relief flooded Mrs. Crawford's face. "Thank you. Come and visit sometime, Ruby. You, too, Mrs. Bindle."

"Yes, ma'am," Ruby said.

"Excuse me," Mrs. Crawford added, looking very uncomfortable. "But, Mrs. Bindle, you aren't on your way right this minute, are you?"

"I am." Marie turned in the road and tucked her hair behind her ear.

"But you aren't—dressed." Concern washed over her face.

Marie looked down. "Oh my. I'm still in my nightgown, aren't I?"

"Mrs. Marie, it looks like you're wearing your palate with all that paint on you. It'll never wash out." Ruby snickered but quickly stopped when she saw how upset Mrs. Marie was.

"Then I'll toss it." Marie ran back toward the house and disappeared inside.

For several minutes, Ruby stood in silence, looking at the ground instead of at Mrs. Crawford, not sure what to say. Finally, the woman broke the awkward silence.

"Ruby, how is Mrs. Bindle doing?" Mrs. Crawford stepped toward her.

"Just fine, ma'am. Just normal, like every day." Ruby shrugged.

"Is Mr. Bindle home?"

"No, ma'am. He's gone for a bit. Newspaper business."

"Is there food in the house for you?"

"Yes. Mr. Frank made sure we were packed full before he set out."

"Well, I will leave you then. If you need anything, come to Solomon Hill. People know where we live. Just ask anyone for our house, you hear?"

"Yes, ma'am."

"Ruby, this is important. Come for me if you need me."

"Bye now, Mrs. Crawford. Thank you again for the hair oil." Ruby hoped her words would scoot Mrs. Crawford on her way.

Marie emerged from the house, buttoning her dress and hurrying across the porch.

"Ready, Mrs. Marie?"

Marie nodded and walked right past Ruby without saying a word. She grabbed the handle of the wagon started at a fast pace as though she was running from her discomfort. Ruby had to hurry to catch up.

They had walked a fair distance when Marie said, "I am so sorry if I embarrassed you in front of Mrs.Crawford."

"Not embarrassed. I'm just glad the voices made the

suggestion of finding something to paint. I just think it would have been polite of them to also say you needed to change before leaving the house."

Marie slowed her pace and smiled. "Let's kick off our shoes. Toes get too stuffy inside of shoes. They need fresh air just like our noses."

"How do you get toenails to look like that?"

"Painted red? Would you like painted toenails too?"

"Oh please!"

Marie plopped down in the grass and pulled off the lid to the red paint. Taking a small brush, she dipped the tip into the color and stroked each nail one by one until all ten gleamed bright red.

Ruby waited for her nails to dry. "I have a question, Mrs. Marie."

"I might have the answer." Marie held her head up and closed her eyes as the wind came sweeping past.

"When the Crawfords' home was taken, why did they move to Solomon Hill? Why not stay in town where Mr. Crawford didn't have to go so far to work?"

"There wasn't any other place available to them. And they couldn't pack up and leave Denton, as so many others did; they own a business here. There's a farmer by the name of Mr. Miles who sold 35 acres of his own land to negroes—those who wanted to stay, that is. It's a sad time for Denton. Not sure if our town will ever heal."

"People will forget. Forgetting causes healing."

"Maybe. It will take lots of time, and maybe generations to heal this open wound." Marie grew silent as she looked about the prairie.

"Mrs. Marie? Are you feeling alright?" Ruby had grown concerned over her long silence.

Marie shook herself. "I'm fine. Thank goodness my voices aren't too bad out here. In town, it's all I heard." Marie looked down at her hands on her lap, as though she were ashamed of them.

"Are the voices good ones, Mrs. Marie?"

"Sometimes they are. But—enough of this kind of talk for today. Your toenails have dried. Come on. Let's paint."

Along the dirt road, Ruby was so proud of her painted toenails that she had an awful time keeping herself from constantly looking down. Finally, Marie excitedly announced, "That's it! Let's paint that!"

There ahead was a rolling meadow jam-packed with wild flowers with the sky above chock-full of cotton-tufted clouds. In the distance, an old red barn tilted to its side.

Marie set up her easel while Ruby took the lids off the paints. Ruby watched Marie wet her paper, and just as it was about to be dry, she splashed the top with Paynes gray paint and the bottom with ochre yellow. The two blended together in the center becoming an ominous shade of green. Love ruled Marie's life. It showed up in her paintings, in her laughter, and in the way she explained things to Ruby.

"I'm doing watercolor today. And this is the way the sky looks just before a fierce storm."

Ruby sat at the edge of the wagon, stuffing tomato sandwiches and cold roast beef into her mouth as Marie displayed her palate of colors.

"Next, the land in viridian and flowers in colors of alizarin crimson, cobalt blue, ultramarine violet, and cadmium yellow." The barn was the last to be painted in crimson and black.

"What do you think of it?" Marie asked, stepping away from the canvas.

"Mrs. Marie, I think your sky looks just like that sky." Ruby pointed beyond the canvas. Sure enough, the same ominous green color spread across the horizon.

"Oh my. You haven't started your picture yet, but there's no time for it now with that storm coming. Ruby, close your eyes and take a deep breath."

Ruby did as she was told.

"Tell me the fragrance."

"Rain. It smells like rain."

"We better head home fast!" The two hurried to reload the wagon with Marie's tools, leaving behind remaining bits of food for birds, squirrels, and coyotes. They hurried back down the hill and several dirt roads, reaching the house just in time. As they carried the wagon up to the shelter of the porch, the sky opened, and rain poured over the roof, sounding like hundreds of people beating it with a hammer.

Unexpectedly, Marie dashed like a jackrabbit from the cover of the porch out into the viridian-colored grass. She held her arms out and threw her head back inviting the deluge of rain pouring from the sky. She glistened and sparkled from head to barefoot toes. In an instant, she was soaked with rain through her clothes to her skin. Ruby watched the woman who seemed suddenly and strangely free until it stopped raining.

Hours later, both slept soundly in their beds.

28

The next evening, they devoured cucumber sandwiches.

Barefoot, Marie carefully balanced on the porch's wood hand railings to hang wind chimes from the rafters. Once that was complete, she set pots of mint on the steps and watered them. The honeysuckle had wound its fingers several feet up the porch supports in the few weeks Ruby had lived there. As the quiet country evening progressed, they sat in rockers, and the wind blew nature's perfume straight into their nostrils and ruffled their skirts.

Marie picked up her pad and began to sketch Ruby with a small burnt willow branch. Shading overlapped, and the essence of Ruby evolved. When the annoyance of the mosquitos became a constant, they abandoned the porch and sat in the parlor after changing into nightgowns. Marie sang along with a song on the radio: "(I'll Be With You) In Apple Blossom Time."

"You're much better at drawing than I am."

"That's because I've had more years of practice than you."

"I've only drawn with sticks in the dirt."

Marie's involuntary laugh turned to a snort as she handed Ruby paper along with her own piece of burnt willow. Ruby slid the black across the white page creating lines. Never before had she drawn on paper—and she found this to be so much better, so lasting. Eventually, she held up her picture to show Marie and asked, "What do you think?"

"Oh Ruby, you drew Andy. Look at how you captured the light in his eyes. And his hair." Marie's throat went dry. "We have to frame this and hang it in your room."

"May I try oil?" Ruby asked timidly, fingering the brushes and eyeing the paint.

"In time. What do you want to draw next?" Marie spread wax paper across the dining room table then plopped white paper on top of that, followed by tubes of paint, crystal glasses filled with water for dipping brushes, and paint clothes.

Ruby settled into a chair to sketch, but found it too confining. She stood up and leaned over the table. "I want to draw my face, just like you did on the porch."

Marie took a pencil and quickly drew a light outline on her paper. "Let me show you. See, your face narrows at the jaw line. I would say it's heart shaped." She looked from the paper to Ruby and then back again. She watched as Ruby drew a large heart on her paper. "Now, your eyes are almond shaped," Marie said, guiding Ruby's hand. She allowed Ruby to finish it herself.

Ruby stepped back and looked at it, still not convinced it was right. "What does my nose look like?"

Marie thought for a moment and then dashed into the kitchen, returning with a berry and plopped it on the table in front of her.

Ruby laughed, "Does my nose really look like that?"

"Come, let me show you." Marie grabbed Ruby by the hand, and they ran down the hallway into the bathroom. There was a small mirror above the sink, and Ruby stood in front of it to study her face.

"See, your nose is shaped like a small berry—nice and firm, too. Your lips are even and wide. Your eyebrows are short and thick above your eyes," Marie said, outlining Ruby's face and features with her finger. Then, she threaded her fingers through Ruby's hair and raked it straight back. "You are so very beautiful. Yes, let's try those oils."

Ruby blushed. They went back to the dining room where Ruby continued working on her self-portrait. After a bit, Ruby paused. "What color do I use for my skin?"

"Skin tones are not one exact color. They can be tricky." Marie studied Ruby's arm and face. "I would say you are a warm brown. We can mix Vandyke brown with a bit of burnt umber. Your hair is definitely black, and your eyes are a deep brown, so you will need sepia for that. For your lips, we shall lighten some burnt umber."

Ruby made mistakes by adding too much oil in places, causing the picture to become gloppy in a few areas, but the overall effect was very pretty. Marie pronounced it "Fabulous!"

Ruby held up her arm next to Marie's. "Tell me, what skin color are you?"

"Since I'm Italian, I have an olive skin tone, and my hair is blue black. And see my eyes? They're violet."

For hours, they drew, tore up what they drew, went to the refrigerator for more food, and drew more. It seemed they had been at work only a short time when Ruby looked out the window and saw the pink sun coming up over the green corn. "Mrs. Marie! We painted all night."

"Hum, fancy that! Creativity knows no time of day or night."

"I better clean this up so we can get to bed." Ruby began gathering papers.

"Get to bed? We will only wake up again and start all over!"

Ruby reached for a glass, but feeling light-headed from fatigue, she accidentally tipped it over, spilling murky paint water all over the table and onto the floor. It had been such a good night, why did she have to go and spoil it all? Ruby looked at Marie. "I am so sorry!" Ruby blinked back tears and felt her heart beating quicker in her chest.

Marie laughed. "Accidents happen. No need to get upset, Ruby. We'll just clean it up in a moment. But now comes the best part: displaying our artwork." Marie dug out fat thumbtacks from a kitchen drawer, and they hung their paintings all along the stairway wall as they went up the steps to bed.

Marie could be so puzzling.

29

Marie put off going into town for a full week. But with dwindling paints and art paper, there were two choices: stop painting or go to town for fresh supplies. They chose the latter. Marie and Ruby walked barefoot down the dusty road, shoes in hand.

Lately Marie seemed more and more tired—making her forgetful and disoriented at times. Ruby worried that Marie might lose her mind to the voice in her head. *It's important to get a good night's sleep especially while Frank is gone,* Ruby thought. She didn't want him to come home and think everything had gone to seed around the place.

"I guess we better put our shoes on before going into the store," Marie said slowly while standing in front of Hanover's. Marie took a breath, "I just hate shopping. People watch me and snatch my thoughts."

"Mrs. Marie, that's impossible."

"Is it? How come I forget things?"

"Shopping is something I can do for you from now on, Mrs. Marie. If you make a list of items, I'd be more than happy to do the shopping." Ruby finished putting on her shoes and noticed Marie hadn't begun to slip hers back on.

"Are you sure you're ready to do this?" Marie asked.

Ruby nodded enthusiastically. "You can count on me, Mrs. Marie."

"Ruby, thank you!" Marie grabbed Ruby and held her tightly. "Okay. I will sit right here, and you can go in and get these things on my list." Marie pulled the paper from her pocketbook and handed that along with some money to Ruby. "Count the coins out one by one into Mr. Hanover's hand. Alright?"

Ruby nodded and walked into the store and right up to the counter. "Excuse me, Mr. Hanover?"

The clerk, who was stacking dry goods, turned around. "Yes?"

"I want a big, fat sketch pad and these colors. It's all printed right on this for you." Ruby passed him the list. "Oh, and two drawing pencils, please sir."

The clerk adjusted his spectacles and went to work filling the order. He kept gazing from Ruby who patiently stood at the counter to Marie who remained outside on the stoop in front of the store, wiping her brow.

"Is she alright? She looks like the day has done her in."

"She has a churning stomach, I believe." Ruby said, making up a reason.

When the order had been filled and put into a brown paper bag, Ruby counted the coins into his hand just as Marie had instructed.

Mr. Hanover gave another sideways glance at Marie, and then he leaned over the counter to ask in a whisper, "If you aren't a servant, what do you do at the Bindles all day?"

Ruby thought it an odd question but nonetheless smiled broadly, thinking this might be the perfect time to give him a snoot full of her fried legs story. It'd served him right for his nosiness. It'd also be fun to see the look of horror cross his face. But she thought better of it. Perhaps it was time for a whole new story, a prettier story, one that involved her sitting on a throne and eating cookies all day long as Mrs. Marie painted her toenails red.

Something stopped Ruby from saying that, too—it was an inner feeling of separating what was right from what was wrong. She didn't exactly know what that feeling was since her conscience hadn't shown up much before she started attending church. But learning about God's ways in church and knowing Myna was probably still praying for her, maybe it was time to be better. Once, saying something that wasn't true only reflected on her. It was her small way of paying folks back for meanness. Now, what she said and did reflected on the Bindles. So Ruby opted for the truth: "We eat all day and draw pictures all night. When there's a chance, we close our eyes to rest them for a bit and eat little sandwiches."

In a second, Marie was off the front stoop, through the door, and up at the counter. "What are you saying to Ruby?" She slammed the shoes she held in her hand up on the counter. "Huh?"

Aghast, Mr. Hanover took a step back and stammered, "I— I was just wondering, wh— what your servant did all day long."

"*Servant?* You call Ruby a *servant?* You've got a lot of nerve! We do not believe in servants." Marie picked up the store bell from the counter and tossed it across the room. She snatched up the bag of art supplies along with her shoes. "Come, Ruby!"

Marie fumed as they walked home. "He has no call humiliating you like that."

"He didn't humiliate me—he's just used to things being one way, and when they're a different way, it confuses him. Mrs. Marie, forgive me for saying so, but you've gone and shed a bad light on your name."

"As if I care." A storm brewed in Marie's violet eyes.

"Don't be hard on others. It's bound to keep coming up."

Marie looked into her young face. "It still isn't right."

"Don't you see? The only thing that matters is what's real."

"You teach me so much, Ruby." Marie suddenly smiled.

They kept walking down the road, but Ruby could tell by Marie's expression that she had no intention letting go of her anger toward Mr. Hanover, so Ruby decided to do whatever it took to quell Marie's nerves. Maybe stirring up a pitcher of sweet tea would be helpful in making that happen.

For now, Ruby kept quiet. They'd walked in silence for a mile when they reached a bend in the dirt road, and someone jumped out of the bushes. Marie closed her eyes and screamed, turning her back.

Ruby faced the person who jumped out at them. She wasn't impressed. But Marie still had her eyes shut.

"What should we do, Mrs. Marie?"

"Prepare to run," Marie squealed.

"I think Louie is the one who should prepare to run."

Marie opened her eyes and swirled about. "Oh, it's

you, Louie. Sorry if I gave you a start." Now she laughed at herself.

"I'm just fine, ma'am. I didn't see you there. Just Ruby." He tipped his new cap. "Just clowning around."

"Lunatic." Ruby muttered.

"Are you enjoying your stay at the Clarks'?" Marie dropped her shoes and folded her hands quietly in front of her dress. She seemed so suddenly calm that Ruby figured the scream did her some good. "Upright people, they are."

"They're fine. Thank you for asking." His smart reply made Ruby's jawline slack.

"With your permission, Mrs. Bindle, I'd like to talk to Ruby. It'll only be for a moment."

"Ruby, how do you feel about that?" Marie asked.

Curious, Ruby said, "I guess it would be alright if we sat on the front porch where you can keep an eye on us."

"Good. I'll set out cool drinks for you both. I may have some peanut butter cookies in the cookie jar, too. Would you like to have some?"

"Yes, ma'am. I'd like that a lot." His hand flexed at his side.

Marie slipped back into her shoes. "Come along then."

30
.....

Ruby chewed her lip. For the next few minutes, she didn't speak. Louie seemed content to sit peacefully for a bit. There was no doubt Ruby had plenty to say, but she kept it bottled up for the time being. For the moment, she leaned on the railing and kept both eyes on Louie who made himself right at home on the front porch swing and helped himself to three glasses of lemonade and a plateful of cookies that Marie had baked for *her*. He looked like a brand new person in neatly pressed pants and a shirt that was carefully buttoned down the front, no missing buttons.

Finally, Ruby broke the silence: "I don't want no trouble from you, Louie. Tell me quick: what d'you want to talk about?" Ruby stared at him for a few seconds longer than needful, making him squirm a bit. Marie peeked out the window at them.

"I seen you wallowing in your grief. I'm sorry about Andy." He gazed at her under his low-slung hat and looked her dead in the eyes. She could have thought of a hundred ways to argue with him but Ruby never expected him to mention Andy's name. Her hand itched to hit him for it.

"You can drop the lies with me. I'm the only one in this town who knows who you really are."

"Who do you think I am?"

"You're the one who hit me over the head with a block of wood and snatched my food back in New York City. You're the one who pushed an elderly lady down in the street and took her purse. You're the one who killed Red and then tried to drown me in a stream. You're the one—"

"Okay, okay, okay."

"I want you to stay away from me and the Bindles, you hear?"

"You sure are feisty." He walked to Ruby and gave her shoulder a shove.

"And you ain't nothing but than a pathetic waif—just like me," Ruby said with stinging bitterness. She balled her hands into fists, seething with fury. "Ever since you moved into the Reverend's house, you've put on airs. But you're the same mean person you always were. You ain't changed. I know it. And soon everyone else will know it, too."

"What're you gonna do about it?"

"Nothing. I don't have to do a single thing. You'll do it all on your own."

"Things are different here for me. And I want you to know that I really am sorry about Andy. From now on, I'll stay away from you." Louie was done talking now. He'd apparently said what he needed to say. Louie returned her gaze for a moment and then turned away.

Ruby was confused because she didn't see any hatred in him or the mischief that had always been there. Didn't matter, though. Soon, he bounced down the steps of the gray house and took long strides across the yard in the direction of his home.

Ruby wrapped her arms around the porch post to watch him go. She figured Louie might just be trying to clear his guilty conscience. She hated to admit it, but there was something different about him today. And he did seem sorry about Andy. But it didn't matter if he repented until this time next year; she'd never forget what he did. Hating him made the pain of Andy's death bearable, and it kept her on her guard to prevent a surprise attack. In spite of that, she took back wishing he had died in place of Andy; instead, she just wished Andy had lived.

Ruby picked up Louie's empty plate and glass and pushed in through the screen door to find Marie washing the kitchen floor.

"What did Louie want?" Marie asked, wringing out a washrag in a bucket of water. By then, she had changed into a pair of Frank's jeans which sat low on her hips and were rolled up to her knees.

"Nothing." Ruby set the plate and glass on the counter next to the sink.

"It didn't seem like nothing to me. I'd think you'd want to be friends with him since you came out here together."

"Friends? Don't you know a lunatic when you see one?" Ruby snorted.

Marie rocked back on her heel and looked up at Ruby, answering softly, "No, but I know an angel when I see one."

Just when Ruby was at her worst, out came Marie's love for her, strong and powerful. Ruby's conscience clobbered her worse than a piece of wood.

"Let me help you, Mrs. Marie."

"That's great, but first, hand me the clean rag, will you? This one is all dirty now. We got a lot of paint on this floor that only close inspection and a lot of elbow grease can get up." Marie folded the wet rag and then tossed it toward the sink, but it hit a cupboard, and the extra water splashed Ruby's dress. "Oops." Marie giggled.

Still turning over her conversation with Louie inside her head, Ruby wiped her bodice with a dry towel. Then, she took a clean rag from the drawer. Half-heartedly, she tossed it at Marie, but her aim was bad, and it plunked into the middle of the bucket of water, splashing Marie. Ruby's heart stopped, and her body froze.

Marie wiped her face off with the bottom of her blouse and then rung the extra water onto the floor. Next, she reached down into the bucket for the rag and without even ringing it out flung it back toward Ruby who ducked. The rag hit a plate that was hanging on the wall, breaking it.

"Oh, Mrs. Marie, that was such a pretty rose plate!"

A smile crept across Marie's face, and she scooped out a handful of water and flung it at Ruby. Not knowing if this would suffice for her punishment, Ruby didn't flinch.

Marie sighed. "Ruby, we're in a water fight, and you look so serious! This is supposed to be fun. Now smile and throw water at me!"

Ruby grinned. Within seconds, water dripped from the walls and covered the floor. Unexpectedly, Frank walked into the kitchen in the middle of their fight.

"Do we have leaky pipes?" He laughed and offered a fresh bouquet of blue bonnets to Marie who sprang from the floor and hugged his neck.

"It's so good to have you home," Marie said, wildly kissing his cheeks.

"And how is my other girl?" Frank winked at Ruby over Marie's shoulder.

"Fine. Your other girl is just fine," Ruby said softly, water dripping from her chin.

"I have a gift for you, too, Ruby." Frank unsnapped the locks on his suitcase and raised the lid.

There they were. Two specially made shiny shoes with a built-up sole on one. An expensive pair, she figured. Ruby eagerly put them on, and Frank helped her walk around the house until she was steady on her feet.

Now, Ruby flung her arms around Frank's neck. "Thank you, Mr. Frank! I don't limp no more. I can walk my old walk now!"

As Ruby drifted off to sleep, she thought about how good it felt to belong to a family. She listened to the sound of typewriter keys pounding paper and breathed in the perfume of Marie's paint that filled the air as the colors of her flowers on canvas turned from pretty colors to brown.

31
....

A week later, life flipped upside down.

Ruby was dressed and downstairs as Frank started breakfast. As normal, Marie's newest painting was taped to the wall. Ruby paused to look in admiration. How odd—it was only partially complete. Marie never hung an unfinished piece. Centered on the paper were prairie flowers of Autumn Indigo, but instead of blue, they were brown and shriveled.

Ruby couldn't stop staring. A weird feeling slid up her spine.

It was then she noticed Marie and Frank were speaking in hushed tones in the corner of the room. Marie was a frightful mess with unkempt hair and still wearing the same dress she had worn for the past two days.

"Oh, Ruby, there you are. Have a seat at the table, dear. You know, I was just thinking what a special day Sunday is to me. I love making breakfast for you and Marie. And I thought, 'It's only Tuesday, but let's break with tradition, and I'll cook today, too.'" Frank turned off the stove and carried the griddle of food to the table. "You never know what a day will bring."

The beginnings of this day had a whole new ring to it. Gone was the banter and the laughter about doughy pancakes. They ate mainly in silence. Frank looked sadly at Ruby while Marie kept staring out the window.

Just as breakfast finished, the very moment Ruby always feared might come sooner or later, finally showed up in the form of Mrs. Crawford. Frank and Marie didn't seem surprised to see her at their front door. All four of them sat together in the parlor. No cold drinks or plates of cookies were offered, but there was plenty of awkward silence to go around. The sound of the mantle clock seemed to grow louder and louder with each passing moment.

"The oil you gave me for my hair works well. Thank you, Mrs. Crawford," Ruby finally said, trying to liven things up. She looked down at her fingernails. They were clean.

Marie was the next to talk. "Ruby, schools starts in a matter of days. Are you looking forward to making new friends?"

Ruby didn't care if she made friends or not, but she smiled with false sincerity. "I don't care."

"Don't you want friends?" Mrs. Crawford asked.

"Excuse me for repeating myself, but I really don't care."

"Ruby, have you noticed I don't have friends?" Marie asked.

"You have Mrs. Crawford over there."

Mrs. Crawford smiled.

"I am looking forward to learning."

"How nice. She must be a smart one." Mrs. Crawford leaned forward.

"Since you have come here to live, you must have noticed how divided the town is on certain issues." Frank tapped his knee with his fingers.

"I noticed straight off the very first day. But it was also that way in New York."

"We've had conversations about this. I imagine it's confusing." Frank cleared his throat.

"You talking about Solomon Hill and some people saying I'm your servant?"

"Yes," Frank answered, "precisely."

"They don't understand our situation. I'm fine with it. Don't matter what others think, just what we know is true." Ruby narrowed her eyes at Marie whose tangled hair needed a good brushing.

"Ruby, I want people to know the exemplary young girl that you are and not be regarded as a servant living with Frank and me. I want so much more for you. The good Lord knows you've had your share of heartbreak in this life. I will sacrifice anything for you to be seen as a girl with promise. I would even give up my own happiness to make you happy," Marie spoke emotionally. The wind played melodies on the porch chimes. Slowly, Marie pulled a flowered handkerchief out of her pocket and dabbed at the corners of her eyes.

"There are different schools here. One for blacks and one for whites," Mrs. Crawford said, "just like any other town around here."

"I suppose." Ruby shrugged. "Even though I came a long distance, I still haven't been many places."

"You need to go to the school meant for you," Marie continued. "The black school. I know up north many of the schools are no longer segregated, but the south takes longer to get things done."

"Mrs. Marie, I'm not so sure what 'segregated' means, though."

"Segregated means the white community is separate from the black community. We have different schools, drinking fountains, areas where we live, for some examples," Marie continued.

"For you to live here with us, it might confuse you," Frank said.

"I don't get confused that easily, Mr. Frank." Ruby cocked her head to one side as she always did when she tried figuring out certain matters. "What are you saying, Mrs. Marie? Mr. Frank?"

"Lately, I've had a lot of difficult days." Marie wiped her nose with a hankie.

"You talking about your voices?" It seemed to Ruby that Marie kept changing what she wanted to say.

Ruby watched Marie's hand tighten around her hankie. Her face paled. She kept swallowing hard as though trying to say words that weren't coming into her head. "Exactly. My voices. They come and go. Sometimes, I get confused by them. There are people in this town who don't understand me because of them."

"I know just what you mean, Mrs. Marie. There are people who misunderstand me all the time." Ruby tried to comfort her. "They say things about me as well."

"I feel like I'm living on the outside of things." Marie said.

"I didn't think that mattered to you, Mrs. Marie. I'm sorry." Ruby took her hand.

"I don't want that for you. Living on the outside. People don't know how to receive you because you're not our servant. And they don't accept that you're our child."

"I know."

"But living with us, you will always feel as though you are on the outside of things—both from living with white people and because of my voices. I want more for you because I love you. Ruby, if there was another way, another road, another path, I would take it. And it's time we stop thinking of ourselves and do what is best for you. We need to set you on your road."

"What're you saying?" Ruby now looked hard at Mrs. Crawford. Was this her doing?

"For now, until I'm better or until people become more progressive in thought, you will stay with the— the Crawfords over on Solomon Hill."

Ruby doubled over in instant pain at the thought of leaving Marie, Frank, the gray house, and the wind that skipped around in the yard like a child. There were also Andy's sailboats on the walls and his butterflies in the garden that occasionally came inside to remind Ruby that life was beautiful. She was losing it all.

Anger welled. Distrust returned. "Why'd you tell me I belonged here only to send me away? If love means caring for someone, how can you tell me you love me one day and then send me somewhere else the next? I was pushed out of a life with my mother, a life with Mama Burke, and a life at the orphanage with Myna. Now that I finally have a loving home, how can you push me out of it just because outsiders don't understand?"

"This is for the best right now." Marie's eyes pleaded for understanding. "It's not just the outsiders."

There was no strength left in Ruby. Her heart broke more with every breath she took. She began hiccupping disjointedly, and large tears rolled down her face, enough to wet her dress.

"Let me stay. I can take care of you, Mrs. Marie. I will be your servant and not your child. I will work until midnight and be up before dawn. Just don't send me away! I can't never become the person I'm meant to be away from this house that holds my strength."

Frank moved to comfort Ruby with a hug, but she didn't really want to be comforted right then, so she shrugged away.

"Marie's illness is more than a girl can manage," he said.

"I've managed harder things." Ruby stood her ground.

"You'll have a calmer, better, more ordered life with the Crawfords."

A better life? What could possibly be better than falling to sleep after Mr. Frank saying goodnight prayers, oversleeping until 8 am, and finding Mrs. Marie painting one of her stories? Her heart thumped hard in her chest. Gasping for air, she looked down at her shaking hands. When she opened her mouth to protest, she couldn't find her voice. For the first time in her life, Ruby was shocked into silence. The rush of adrenaline was gone, leaving her weak.

Marie had little to add other than that Ruby would be leaving with Mrs. Crawford that day. School would start in a few days, and they wanted her settled by then.

It was much too late to set the day right. As Ruby climbed the steps with Marie to pack her belongings, she went numb. She had reached her emotional peak and bottom within the matter of a few moments. Ruby had been angry, hurt, confused, frustrated, loved, and unloved all at the same time. It was too much to feel all at once, so instead, she felt nothing. Her heart and head only felt empty.

Marie neatly folded Ruby's clothes into the suitcase while Ruby went to dusting the room, saying goodbye to it in her own way. When Marie reached into the closet for the last dress, the blue one with the ivory buttons, Ruby stopped her.

"No, Mrs. Marie, leave just one dress. It gives me hope I'll get to come back. Today is only a temporary setback from what's meant to be. You'll see that for yourself in time. Sending me away is a mistake."

"I hope you're right, Ruby."

Marie gave her such a look that Ruby knew there was something more in sending her away than what had been said. Ruby went down the steps and out the back door into the garden where the easel still stood with a blank sheet of paper clipped to it. With her eyes closed, she smelled the scent of prairie flowers. She turned around and looked at the gray house surrounded by vines and butterflies. Ruby drew a picture of it all in her mind while trying to understand how adults could make such wrong decisions. Then, she sucked in a long breath, locking in the moment.

Having no control over the business of prayer, seeing as her prayers weren't being answered, she went home with the Crawfords and waited for God to move in His mysterious way—as Reverend Clark said each Sunday. Or until everyone came to their senses, whichever happened first.

32

Ruby tried not to cry, but she could not resist the tears. She pressed her face into the pillow on her new but worn bed in the home she wanted no part of. Through the wall, she heard James and Joel complain about having to share a room because of their new sister. She stared out the window for hours at nothing in particular. Ruby knew she was loved. She had yearned for it her entire life, and now that she finally had it, she felt she had a twisted dose of it, tearing her between two families. Thoughts of the parted twins, Emily and Amy, returned.

Early evening, Mrs. Crawford invited her to dinner, but Ruby turned her back. She felt ill and feared she'd topple over if she tried to stand. Like a rock, she lay immobile, and her brown eyes roamed the cracks in the ceiling, wondering if she'd ever have anyone in her lifetime to call her own. Now she knew. Eventually, everyone would leave her, one by one. It all began the day she lost her mother. She lost the Burkes, Myna, Mrs. Perkins (although she was really happy about that one). Then she lost Marie and Frank. Worst of all, she lost Andy. Inevitably, she would somehow lose the Crawfords, too. The one thing Ruby knew was that she didn't want anyone to tell her they loved her ever again. It hurt too much when they took it back. Ruby patted her chest harder and harder, willing herself to become tough, to never love anyone ever again.

"I'm building a wall, building a wall. I will stay strong. I will get through this. I will not love again. I am indomitable."

Hunger finally drove Ruby from bed. She followed voices into the kitchen where her new family sat around the table finishing dinner. Ruby kept her head down and sat at the only empty chair. Mrs. Crawford ate primly. In fact, the whole family ate dinner in perfect politeness with words like "please" and "thank you" in nearly every sentence.

"Ruby, we're pleased you are here," Mrs. Crawford said finally.

"Thank you, ma'am." Ruby scooped potatoes and a pork chop onto her plate. She took a big bite of each and admitted to herself it tasted better than Marie's cooking. But Mrs. Crawford had far more years of practice at getting it right.

When she'd finished eating, Ruby looked around at the kitchen. It was neat as a pin. There were no vases of dead or fresh flowers all over the place, no piles of things waiting to be sorted, for everything was already organized—sorted and orderly, as if chaos had been expelled from this house.

At Marie's house, chaos was the silent guest that left traces everywhere. There was dust over all the furniture, and there were piles of to-be's: a pile to be organized, a pile to be straightened, and a pile to be tossed out. Ruby missed the disarray. Every bit of it. Perhaps some of Reverend Clark's words last Sunday were true: that everyone learned lessons from one another. What could she teach the Crawfords? What would she learn from them?

The first night seemed to last forever. Ruby wanted no more luck. She wanted no good luck or bad luck, no highs or lows. She wanted peace without fear of loss. Ruby understood that she'd already had more than her fair share of loss yet should expect more to come. Nonetheless, Ruby felt ready.

33

It was the first day of school. Ruby rode next to Mr. Crawford as he drove the horse-pulled wagon, and the boys sat in the back next to fresh produce. "Have you ever been to school, Ruby?"

"Never. I'm a bit confused about this day." Ruby held a sack lunch on her lap.

"It's a one-room schoolhouse. Two teachers. Most only have one teacher. Just do what the teachers tell you, and all will be fine." He chewed on the lip of his pipe while holding reins with one hand.

"Yes, sir. Mr. Crawford, did you go to school?"

"I did, Ruby. I even have a teaching degree from a black college—but that college caught fire and burned to the ground some years ago."

"Then why aren't you a teacher?"

"If you have a degree and still can't get work, then you need to re-evaluate. I opened my grocery store, and it's doing just fine. I may not be the richest man, but we won't go hungry either. We can't afford electricity like the Bindles and other white folk, but we do alright. Come next summer, you can help out at the store, if you'd like. I could use your help."

"I'd like that very much." Ruby smiled thinking about working in a room filled with food. Certainly Red would be pleased.

"A few years from now, the boys will go off to college. You might like to take the business over from me."

Ruby had no thoughts on the matter. Her thoughts only went as far as today.

It wasn't long before they reached the once-red clapboard schoolhouse that had long-since mellowed into a rich pink color after years of baking in the sun.

Slowly, Ruby got down from the wagon and walked steadily into the classroom, where she stood at the back and looked around. The ceiling came to a point like a church. Long wooden tables sat in precise rows stretching from one side of the room to the other with chairs placed neatly behind them. This was her first time inside of a school. The black teachers, Miss Collins and Miss Jackson, told the children where to sit. Miss Jackson guided Ruby to a chair in the very back with other students who looked about her age.

The little ones were seated in the front, and the older ones got seats in the back. The teachers took turns explaining how the school term worked and what the expectations were. At first, Ruby didn't listen. There was a book in front of her whose contents were mesmerizing. Slowly she turned the pages as reverently as Reverend Clark turned the pages of his Bible. It was a book filled with numbers and story problems. School would be a good thing. And then Miss Jackson said electrifying words that snatched her attention:

"There's a new growing cultural movement among the black community."

Ruby closed her book.

"As you know, we were all moved here to Solomon Hill. Many of those who chose not to do so migrated north to cities where there are opportunities for work and freedom."

"Where up north is this movement happening?" Ruby cut in.

Every student turned around in their seat and looked at her.

"I'm not here from Solomon Hill. I'm from New York City, north of here."

Miss Jackson smiled. "This artistic negro explosion is happening in Harlem, New York, Chicago, too.

"It's a rebirth of black art forms emerging in the areas of literature, music, painting, fashion, music, and so much more. We will study many of them. It's happening. Along with this are cries for equality and civil rights which are in the forefront right now. We live in exciting times, boys and girls. We get to be a part of it all."

Inspired, Ruby clapped, thinking about how this had been happening in New York and she never knew it until this moment.

Miss Collins stepped in with the rest of the lesson. "We must resist prejudice when it happens to us in any form. At this school, we teach that all men should live in peace with one another. Contend for freedom and equality for every man, woman, and child."

"Excuse me, Miss." Ruby held up her hand.

"Yes?"

"What is equality?"

"Equality is a simple word. It means to be fair. If you can vote, then I can vote, too, no matter what color skin I have or what gender I am."

Miss Jackson added, "Women just got the vote along with negroes. But not everyone takes advantage of that right. I want y'all to grow up and vote. It's a way to raise your voice and be heard."

The words sounded correct and settled in Ruby's spirit as truth.

Completely at peace, she listened to the teachers as they turned their attention to black poets and authors: James Weldon Johnson, Harriet E. Wilson, Jessie Fauset, and Claude McKay to name a few. During recess, no one vied for Ruby's attention, allowing her to sit alone and read.

At the end of the school day, Ruby held her literature book and math book tightly. As soon as she got home, Mrs. Crawford told her to set the table. By dark, Mr. Crawford returned home. He sat in his armchair and said, "I am tired to the bones." This was a man who lacked surprise. He always dressed in the same brown pants with white shirtsleeves rolled back, except on Sundays when he wore black pants with the rolled-up white sleeves to church. Sitting behind his newspaper for an hour after work, he did not utter a single word to anyone but quietly puffed a bit of smoke out of his pipe.

She wanted to share with him what she had learned in school, but he didn't ask. Instead, she waited for him to finish with his newspaper so she could talk about it. Watching his facial expressions as he read an article Frank wrote, Ruby wondered what Mr. Crawford thought. She longed to read what Frank had written. However, she held her tongue because she did not want the Crawfords to think she was ungrateful for their misguided efforts on her behalf. When he'd finished reading, Mr. Crawford rolled it up and stuck it in the trash. He seemed in a hurry to leave the room. Ruby held her words for another day and sprang for the newspaper. Tucked beneath her armpit, she hurried to her room where she stowed it away until after dinner.

Once the dishes were put away, she sat on the edge of her bed scanning the bylines for his name: Frank Bindle. She savored each word.

Below his article, she read another interesting section. The city of Denton was offering a reward of $500 for the capture of Ted T. Grimes, the suspected murderer of a small orphan boy. The man was last seen leaving the train station in a 1920 black Chevy truck. It instructed that any information concerning Mr. Grimes should be reported to the sheriff's office.

"I saw Ted T. Grimes months ago," Ruby said aloud to herself, then quickly looked around to be sure no one had walked past the door to hear.

Love and hatred were two mighty big emotions for an approximately twelve-year-old girl to carry through life. Ruby knew she had to let one go and fill her soul up on the other one. All the church sermons she'd heard of late taught her that forgiveness was crucial to her eternal salvation. To give the words meaning, Ruby decided to practice selective forgiving. It was important to save some to work on later.

Her hatred was toward the Stickman who hurt her and killed Andy. And her hatred was toward Louie who had stolen her lunch, murdered Red, and tried to drown her in the river. Her deepest love was toward Marie and Frank. She had a different kind of feeling toward the Crawfords for wanting her. She loved the Burkes for always—and Myna, too. But the best love was Andy because he had needed her the most. Then there was leftover love, a mysterious fading love for her mother who had always smelled of lavender. Ruby's new life was rich with people who cared about her, black-skinned and white-skinned; they all wanted her for their own. As Myna would say, God's hand brought her here to Texas—even to the Crawfords.

Ruby imagined standing in a field of food. Instead, she was standing in a field of love and affection from two families. Somehow, she was not altogether comforted by it. And when this love was expressed to her, she began to worry.

Hatred and love confused her. Sometimes they ended up as the same emotion. Ruby loved her mother. Yet her mother had abandoned her without food or a place to live. At time, hatred replaced love. And other times, when she recalled her mother's soft voice, love replaced the hate.

Then, there was the matter of forgiveness. She'd have to tackle that one person at a time. Examining all the people who had wronged her, Louie seemed to be more useful to her right then. Tomorrow, she would look for him.

Ruby lay between the covers and looked at her clothes hanging on pegs. Then, her eyes were drawn to starlight outside her window. Ruby thought about all the people she loved. She held Marie's doll close, named them in prayer, and pulled the line-dried sheets up to her neck. *If you are trying to find me, Mother, I am here, and I am well. Goodnight, sweet Mama who smells of paint and whose voice is a song.* Lately, when she thought of her mother, it was no longer a faceless woman in a red coat who swam in the air before her, but was instead Marie.

At the end of the week, after Saturday chores were finished at the Crawfords', Ruby set out for the Reverend's house and found it right where she suspected it to be: next to the church. She had to give Louie the credit he deserved. She had seen him in church and at school, but he had kept his promise and left her alone. He hadn't spoken to her since that day on the porch.

"Hello, Ruby. It's a fine morning. What can I do for you?" Mrs. Clark greeted her at the door.

"I would like to see Louie, please, ma'am."

"Would you like to come in for breakfast?"

"No thank you, ma'am. I just need to say a few words to Louie, and then I'll be on my way."

Mrs. Clark left the door open when she went to get Louie.

It was already hot out. It was hard getting used to this heat still hanging around in the fall. New York would have started to cool by now. Ruby leaned up against a tree and wrapped her arms around herself to calm her nerves about what she needed to say. Louie was still a scary person to her, but she accepted that he may have changed. If her goal was forgiveness, this was a good place to start.

Louie came to the door. His mouth dropped open to see her standing in the yard.

Ruby noticed his hair was mussed, reminding her of the last time she saw Marie. Maybe Louie was given to spells too. That would explain a whole lot.

Louie and Ruby walked down the road, picking up sticks, breaking them apart, and then tossing them to the side.

"How do you like school?" Louie asked

"Good. It never occurred to me that there's so much I don't know. I can't wait until Monday." Ruby gushed with a hop in her step. "Do you like your school?"

"Not much. Everyone there but me can read."

"How long were you on the streets without a home back in New York?"

"I don't remember having a home, not ever." Louie kicked a rock like it had insulted him.

"That's why you can't read. No one taught you."

"Are you saying *you* know how to read?" Louie asked skeptically.

"Yep. I know how to read but not as good as other kids my age." Ruby stopped at a bridge and looked over. She cupped her hand over her eyes for shade. "Never mind about school. You probably wonder why I came to see you."

He nodded.

"I've come to accept your apology."

"Thanks." Louie pulled a long piece of grass out of the ground and placed one end into his mouth to chew.

It was annoying that Louie hadn't anything more to say. She had counted on him to grovel for his past sins so she could take advantage. When it seemed like nothing more was forthcoming, she moved on to the next point of her visit.

"I have a favor to ask of you. But I can't ask it without confessing to you that I wished you dead in Andy's place."

"S'okay," Louie said.

"According to what the Reverend says each Sunday, it's *not* okay. Or haven't you been listening?"

"I listen alright. I've changed, Ruby."

"How've you changed?"

"I don't know. It's hard to explain. I'm not mad anymore. Or scared. I'm— happy. I think it's because of the Clarks. They're nice people."

"I'm glad for you. But truth is I sure didn't like the old you at all. Maybe if I get to know the new you, I'll like you better. Then, I can stop wishing you dead, and my conscience'll be clear."

"Sounds fair."

"Then let's shake hands on it."

"I'm glad you're giving me a chance to be friends," Louie said, shaking Ruby's hand.

"You're welcome. Do you think there's even a little bit of the old Louie that still hangs around inside your soul somewhere?"

"First you tell me you didn't like me when I was bad, and now you're asking me if there's any of that left in me." He narrowed his eyes at her. "What's going on?"

"There's a part of the Louie from the past that would be helpful in the present."

"What part is that?"

"I'm in need of a lunatic's help." Ruby pulled out a wanted poster from her dress pocket. "I found this hanging on a street post on my way over here. This is the man who beat Andy and me. It says his name here is Ted T. Grimes—I call him Stickman—and he beat Andy so hard that it killed him. There's a reward for apprehending him; that means telling the police. I figure, together, we can find him."

Louie smiled. "I think I can conjure up some of the old Louie. Tell me your plan."

"Stickman has to live near here since he showed up the day we arrived in town by train, and I've seen him once since then. You and I were good at finding hiding places in New York."

"Especially me. I could track down anything or anybody," Louie said, beaming.

"I figured you'd be good at this. I'm good at being invisible. People have a habit of walking right past me without seeing me. With your tracking and my invisibility, we can find this Stickman Grimes."

"I notice everything. For instance, I noticed right away that you walk good now."

"Mr. Frank had these made for me." Ruby should Louie her built-up shoes.

"My Reverend Dad bought me a bicycle. Want me to show you how to ride it?"

"Hmm, let me think. Yes, knowing how to ride a bike might come in handy. Louie, want to be partners?"

"Partners."

"Maybe we will be friends a good long while."

"For now, let's take it one day at a time."

34

Mrs. Crawford asked the Bindles for a favor. She felt Ruby needed settling in time with her new family before visits with the Bindles. It was referred to as "adjustment time." Ruby didn't adjust well and felt this more like this was her "ruination time." Reluctantly, the young couple agreed to Mrs. Crawford's request.

Sunday church became Ruby's favorite because it meant she'd see Frank and Marie—and there wasn't anything Mrs. Crawford could do about that since they all attended the same church.

Ruby tried to look beautiful for Marie and Frank so they'd have second thoughts about sending her to live with the Crawfords and snatch her back home. No matter how hard she wished it, Marie never once asked her to sit with them. Every Sunday, Ruby sat on one of the hard benches up in the balcony while Frank and Marie sat in the cushioned pews in the middle of the church, surrounded by white folk. Never once did Ruby take her eyes from them, always waiting for Marie to turn and smile up at her. Ruby always smiled right back, her heart racing and filled with a daughter's yearning.

The bird's-eye view in church suited Ruby just fine because she could clearly see the backs of everyone's heads. If Marie turned her head just so, Ruby could see the outline of her face. She couldn't look eyes away. Ruby recorded each little mannerism in the journal of her heart. By the way Marie shifted on the seat of the hard pew, Ruby could tell Marie's toes needed to be free. The way Frank's hair started to curl around the tops of his ears meant his skin was hot from the day's heat.

How she wanted to go home with them after the service and see Marie's new paintings. Ruby always knew where Frank had been because she read his newspaper articles, but she yearned to hear his personal stories, anecdotes that no one else was privy to. As if hearing Ruby's daydreams, Mrs. Crawford nudged her to pay attention to Reverend Clark's announcement about a bake sale to raise money for an addition to the church. Ruby could only imagine how many cakes it would take to make enough. From the way Mrs. Crawford loved to bake, Ruby was sure she was about to find out—and that she'd have to help.

When church was over, a parishioner tugged at Mrs. Crawford. "How are you and your new daughter getting along?"

"We're doing just fine. She's an answer to my prayers." Mrs. Crawford smiled and nodded her head proudly.

"I'm so happy for you."

"It seems the old servant of the Bindles got traded in to be the new daughter of the Crawfords." Ruby sighed in a pointed manner, which seemed to embarrass Mrs. Crawford.

Marie and Frank lingered just outside the church doors. Ruby pushed her way down from the crowded balcony, hoping to catch them. Beneath the disapproving gaze of Mrs. Crawford, Ruby threw her arms first around Marie and then Frank. Moving to the side of the church away from the dismissed congregation, Marie asked, "Tell us, how was school?"

"Really good. I believe I'm getting a good education. There's a new movement going on up north that we're learning about. There is art and reading and new songs for us to sing together, Mrs. Marie, all done by negroes. And there's something else. It's called equality. I never heard that word before, but it's about being fair to all people."

"Ruby, I want to hear more about it!"

Frank gave Ruby a few coins. "Buy yourself some ice cream next time you go to town."

"I will if you're the one who takes me to town."

"Oh Ruby, I had no idea it was going to be this hard without you. I thought at least we would get weekly visits." Marie touched Ruby's curly hair.

"Take her." Mrs. Crawford stood a few feet away.

"We— I didn't see you." Marie flushed.

"Take her for the afternoon, but bring her back by supper time." She turned abruptly around and walked off with Mr. Crawford who remained silent.

Back home in the gray house, Ruby ran up the steps to her room and was delighted to find nothing had changed. Even the pillow was still scrunched into a ball where she'd left it. She dropped back onto the bedcovers and closed her eyes, taking in the sounds of the place and the feel of being home again. Several scenarios played in her head. The best one was leaving a note for the Crawfords saying she had decided to return to New York on the very next train—but actually coming home to hide in her closet next to the blue dress or under the bed. Yet that would never work because it would surely panic Marie and Frank until they found her. In the end, the plan would cause needless worry.

Her eyes flew open when she heard Frank call, "Lunch is ready, Ruby!"

She skipped down the steps, holding onto the railing, and banged through the front screen door where the Bindles sat with plates of food: ham, sweet potatoes, green beans with cooked onion and bacon, warm biscuits with honey, and pumpkin pie. Ruby nearly had to pinch herself.

The best part of the day was when they got caught up on their news and Marie showed off her new paintings.

"What do you think, Ruby?"

Ruby looked at each one, taking her time. A void graced each canvas. What was painted seemed muted, neutral, void of natural colors. Not only were the canvases painted in gray tones, but each painting either possessed a missing element or didn't make any sense. In one, bouquets of flowers were held together mysteriously without a vase or a ribbon to hold then that way. In another, a field of dry prairie flowers had clouds baking heat down on them instead of rain reviving them, as one would suspect. The rest were just as bewildering.

Frank called Ruby's name to draw her attention away from what she saw. Then, he regaled both her and Marie with stories about his latest trip to Fort Worth and how he was nearly bitten by a sidewinder. But Ruby was the star of the day. The couple hung on each word she uttered, bewitched by love.

When the day turned to evening, Frank drove Ruby back to the Crawfords' while Marie ran upstairs to cry. All of Ruby's determination never to love again hadn't taken hold. Any minute now, she felt she'd crumble into the pit of sorrow again. Holding the bag of gifts the Bindles had given her, Ruby hugged Frank goodbye and then pulled back to flee into the small house. Ruby hurried into the kerosene lamp light of the living room.

"Ruby, look what I worked on for you all afternoon." Mrs. Crawford held up a mustard yellow and black checkered dress. "You can wear it to school tomorrow."

Ruby heaved a heavy sigh. Black. Her least favorite color to wear.

"Thank you." Ruby couldn't manage a smile and saw impatience briefly cross the woman's face.

"I see you've returned with a bag." Mrs. Crawford did not seem pleased.

"Yes. Mrs. Marie bought some gifts for me."

"Well, let's see them."

Ruby dumped out six art pencils, three ink pens, three oil tubes—red, yellow, and blue—and one sketch pad.

"The Bindles have money to spare for such foolish things while we have five mouths to feed."

"It could have been left at *four* mouths, ma'am." Ruby blinked.

"What can I do to make you happy living with us?" Mrs. Crawford took Ruby's hands.

"I'm not unhappy with you. You try hard to please. It's just, I don't belong here."

"Spoken like a child." The woman waved her hand in the air, dismissing Ruby's words.

"I'm no child. You think you know me, but you don't."

Mrs. Crawford looked quizzically at her.

"When's my birthday?" Ruby asked.

"What?"

"You think I belong here, right? Then you must know when my birthday is. When is it?" Ruby tapped her foot and crossed her arms.

"I guess I don't know." Mrs. Crawford winced.

"July fifteenth, ma'am."

"Ma'am, is it? When will you call me Mother?" Mrs. Crawford sounded exasperated.

Ruby's heart flinched on the words caught in her throat. Mother was the word reserved for her own mother who gave life to her—or for Mama Burke—or Marie who gave her joy.

"But you're not my mother." Ruby saw the hurt in Mrs. Crawford's eyes and decided to meet her halfway. "How about if I call you Ma Elda?"

She nodded as she folded the dress and handed it to Ruby. For the moment, she was pleased. It was a compromise Ruby could live with.

Ruby worked at the kitchen table on her art.

"You should be helping with the cooking," Ma Elda fussed. "Just look at this paint all over my wood table!"

"Sorry." Ruby dropped her chin in guilt. She was ruining the house.

"I see little drops of paint all over the floor, too. 'Sorry' just does not get it with me. But cleaning does!" She tossed a washrag to Ruby that was properly damp and not sopping with water. "And the smell of that paint just makes me sick to my stomach! If I see any more paint marks or if you use another drinking glass to wash your brushes out, I believe I'll scream!" She held up a glass streaked with colors.

Ruby scrubbed the table as hard as she could. Some of the paint came off while others remained. Her cheeks flushed with embarrassment. What a disappointment it must be to wish for a daughter and end up with her.

"All this painting should play second fiddle to your education. As soon as this is cleaned up and dinner is done, we'll have our family devotions. Then, you'll do homework until it's done. Then, prayers and off to bed."

"Yes, ma'am." Ruby was not sure if she wanted her to refer to her as Ma Elda anymore. It would be a relief to her nerves if it had changed back to Mrs. Crawford. The woman was filled with rigid rules to follow, whereas Marie created each moment like wind blowing through the trees. One big thing she noticed about the Crawfords was that they never laughed. Ruby supposed they preferred being sensible.

"I bet you want to be an artist just like your Mrs. Marie." Ma Elda said as she chopped lettuce for dinner. Her movements were as sharp and quick as the knife she used.

"I have a mind of my own and don't need anyone telling me what I'm going to be—or not be. I make up my own mind."

"You watch that tongue of yours, you hear?"

"I hear. I mean no disrespect. But I'm not a skilled painter like Mrs. Marie. And you're an expert cook, but I'll never make tasty dishes like the ones you prepare." Ruby swallowed twice to push down the lump in her throat. "My passion is elsewhere—in the matter of fairness."

"Fairness?" Mrs. Crawford shook her head in confusion.

"Women and negroes may now have the right to vote, but we still don't have equal rights."

"These things take time. Changing people's minds about things doesn't happen overnight."

"I have time." Ruby crossed the room and touched Mrs. Crawford's arm. "It's about passion. Feeling something strong deep down inside. Mrs. Marie is passionate about painting. You're passionate about cooking and baking. I'm passionate about equality."

Mrs. Crawford stared at Ruby as though *she* were a lunatic. After a moment's pause to reflect, a smile crept across her face. "I hear you now. I see I figured many things about you in the wrong way."

"And someday," Ruby said, softening, "I'm going back to New York and to Chicago to meet the authors and poets I've been learning about and to be part of this movement."

"New York *and* Chicago? Well, Miss Ruby Red, if there is a girl anywhere, a black one at that, who can grow up to change things, it'll be you! And I'll be right behind you."

Ruby smiled. Maybe the woman had a good heart buried beneath all her rules.

35

It was the first day of the second week of school. Ma Elda caught Ruby going out the door without her shoes.

"Shoes, young lady." She dangled them in front of Ruby's face. "You can't go limping off to school and arrive there with dirty feet. What will people think of me?"

"Toes are like noses; they need to breathe in the fresh air." Ruby liked to defy the woman even though the shoes made her legs hurt less.

"Shoes! Put them on now."

Ma Elda's words annoyed Ruby, and she scowled while wiggling into the shoes. Ruby walked down the road and listened to the sound of her footsteps. Once out of Ma Elda's view, she yanked the shoes back off again, feeling silt earth between her toes, and didn't care that she limped a bit. It reminded her of being with Marie.

"Mom won't be happy about this!" James warned her.

"Well, then you better not tell her, right?" Ruby could still look mean when she wanted.

"Right," James answered, backing away from her.

"That goes for you, too, right?" she asked Joel.

"What shoes? What toes?" Joel held up his hands in surrender.

Ruby and the boys got to the one-room schoolhouse late. By then, her knee and hip hurt. Maybe defying Ma Elda's orders did her more harm than it made the woman mad. Pride was not a virtue according to Reverend Clark. Ruby took her seat next to the window. At the front of the room was the skinny-legged teacher with her hair pulled back straight and tied into a knot at the back of her head. Miss Collins wore an indigo-striped dress.

"I found out where that Stickman of yours lives,"

Ruby jumped and turned to see Louie leaning in through the window.

"Get out of here or you'll get in trouble."

Louie shrugged. "Can you come out and talk?"

"Shh! No, I can't. I'm in school. *You* should be in school."

"I am in school." Louie grinned.

"*Your* school."

Miss Collins looked up from where she was helping first grade with their math and glanced toward the back of the room. "Whoever is talking, please stop."

"Hang on." Louie snuck into the room through the open door and sat beside Ruby. "I bet no one will notice me."

"Being the only white person in the room, plus the tallest, no, you won't be hard to miss." Ruby held her book to whisper behind. "What were you saying about Stickman?"

"I found out where he lives. It's some shack down a deserted road that dead ends. A few miles outside of town, not too far."

"He should be easy for the police to find then."

"The road is overgrown. Besides, with all the trouble going on in town between the negroes and the whites,

I don't think they care about finding the killer of an orphan boy, not with all the other stuff going on in town." Louie shrugged.

"I care."

"Shhh!" Miss Collins now clapped her hands. She stood up straight when she noticed Louie. "And who are you?"

"Louie, ma'am."

"Have you lost your way?"

"I had lost my way, but Reverend Clark showed me the way."

Ruby and the room began to giggle. Again, Miss Collins clapped her hands for silence as she also stifled a laugh.

"There is a school for you in town with the other white children. This school is for negroes."

"I'm a negro," Louie insisted. "See?" He held out his white arm.

"Enough, Louie. You're white." She tapped her foot with impatience as the class erupted with laughter.

"I am?" He pretended to faint and dropped to the floor.

"Recess!" Miss Collins called and stepped aside as the children raced outside. "Ruby, is he a friend of yours?"

"Yes, ma'am."

"Please take him outside and after recess, I don't want to see him again. Understood?"

"Yes, ma'am."

Louie, apparently fully recovered, followed Rub outside to talk.

"You did a good job of finding him, Louie. After school, let's go to the police."

"No, I want the reward money."

"Reward money? You said you changed. We're going to the police. Now scat before I get in trouble."

After school, Louie rode his bike to town with Ruby sitting on the back fender. When they reached the police station steps, they leaned the bike against the limestone building. With confidence, they walked right through the double front doors of the courthouse. Ruby looked around and thought about the first time she saw the outside of this place. She'd never dreamed of seeing the inside of it.

"Where do we go?" Louie asked Ruby.

"This is my first experience with the jailhouse. You must have some idea what to do after being in the New York one, right?"

"Right!" Louie brightened and squared his shoulders. He walked to the front desk where a large man sat uncomfortably in a small chair. At least Ruby guessed there was a chair somewhere beneath him.

"Excuse me, sir." With trepidation, Louie faced the policeman.

"What is it, boy?" His manner was brisk. When he sniffed, his mustache nearly disappeared up his nostrils, but it came out again as he wiggled his nose.

"I found your murderer."

"Oh, you have, have you? Who?" The man peered up over his reading glasses, duly unimpressed.

"Both of us." He pointed at Ruby and then himself.

"No, I mean which murderer have you two found?" He looked from Louie to Ruby and then back again.

"What's his name again, Ruby?" Louie scratched his head, feeling a bit nervous.

"Grimes. Ted T. Grimes is his name, and his picture is hanging right there on the wall next to you. Look!"

The policeman turned in his seat. "That is a poster of the Grimes fella. You say you've seen this man?"

"Yes, he's hiding near here! I saw him."

The policeman burst out laughing. "Did you now? You've been listening to too much radio! Now skedaddle out of here. I have real work to do." He waved them off.

"But aren't you even going to go out there and arrest him? He killed Andy, a small boy at the train station in June!" Ruby protested, raising her voice.

"Grimes is long gone by now. He sure didn't stick around here after that reward was put on his head. And I don't have time to go chasing after the wild imaginings of a negro and a—hey, aren't you that boy that the Reverend and Mrs. Clark took in?"

"Yes, sir, I am. And I did see Grimes."

The man stared Louie down. "I remember you. You got into some trouble with us when you first came to town. Seems to me, you stole quite a few items from Hanover's. Then you broke out some windows around your neighborhood. The police have been to your house to talk with the reverend about you."

Louie paled. Ruby rolled her eyes. With that kind of history, the police would never believe them.

"Yes, sir. I did all the things you said. I have returned the items and paid for the broken windows. I have not been in any more trouble since then."

"I'm sure. Get out of here you two! Go play your tricks somewhere else." He waved them away again, harder this time.

"But we know where Stickman is!" Ruby cried in fury. How she wanted to take the man by his collar and shake him, but she slid her hands into her pockets instead.

"Stickman?"

"I mean Ted T. Grimes, sir."

"Maybe I should arrest you for mischief!" He lumbered to his feet, acting as though he were about to thrash them across their faces with the back of his hand.

Quickly, Louie and Ruby ran out the door.

"It's better we handle this situation ourselves," Louie said.

"Exactly what I was thinking."

"This Saturday, I'll show you where I saw him."

"How long does it take to get there?"

"Took me a while. With you, I figure it might take a bit longer."

"Come and get me at ten on Saturday morning. I should be done with my chores by then. And remember, don't tell anyone!"

They shook hands in agreement.

36

"Louie, what is it?" Ruby sleepily held open the front door a crack the following morning. Louie looked apprehensive.

"Reverend Dad asked me to come and get you. It's your Mrs. Marie. She's sick with a terrible high fever. The doctor's been with her all night. So has Reverend Dad. Mr. Bindle is out of town."

Having overheard the conversation, Ma Elda said not a word but watched as Ruby hurriedly dressed and tore out the front door. Louie and Ruby rode to the Bindles' on his bike and dropped it on the front steps of the gray house. Ruby hardly noticed the doctor's car out front or the sound of the wind chimes as she entered.

Taking two steps at a time up to the second floor, Ruby knelt beside Marie's bed. Her face looked like that of a porcelain doll with beads of perspiration bubbling on her forehead.

"She's weak," the doctor said. "I've done all I can do for now. I'll be back to check on her in the morning. Someone needs to stay with her."

"I will stay."

"The flu epidemic is sweeping the town."

"It swept New York, too, when I was there."

"I'd stay, but there are other patients to see."

"You go ahead. I'll stay." Her eyes searched Marie's gaunt face for the spirited woman who had laughed in the rain and told off the shopkeeper, but she did not see that woman in this ghostly face that slept far too soundly.

"Very well. The medicine is on the dresser with instructions. Can you read?"

"Yes, of course I can read." Ruby thought of something else. "Doctor, before you leave, I must know what is wrong with Mrs. Marie."

"It's the flu."

"Yes, I know, but there is something else wrong—something that shadows her through life. She hears voices."

The doctor nodded his head. "It's a type of melancholia mixed with a bit of schizophrenia."

"What's that?" Dread crept over Ruby and made shivers run the length of both her arms. She cocked her head to the side.

"Most of the time, Marie is fine, as normal as anyone else. But then there are stretches of time when she becomes unsettled and her mind tangles itself up with wild thoughts. That's when she can't sleep and tends to be up all hours of the night. Soon after, very deep depression and hopelessness engulf her. It gets so bad that she won't speak to anyone, just goes off to bed until it passes. It can take weeks sometimes, months even."

"Is there a cure?"

"No cure, but there are new medicines that ease symptoms. Marie refuses to travel out of town for help, though. She's scared of new people, new places, which is part of the illness."

After the doctor left, Ruby went to the kitchen to make toast with honey in case Marie awoke. As she took the toasted bread from the oven, she noticed a recent picture Marie had painted. It was a bluebonnet shook free of its petals which were now painted brown and curled up on the ground. Ruby tucked the picture under her arm and steadied the tray she took back to Marie's room.

Ruby sat on the floor while Marie slept and went to work on the painting. She brushed over the dried up petals with a violet color to match Marie's eyes. Then, she swept her paintbrush up along the stems making them wider. Choosing a bright shade of blue, Ruby drew the bouquet as though it had been freshly picked. But her form turned out to be awkward and misshapen. It was all wrong. Ruby tore it to pieces.

Birds sang outside the window. Life was all around her as she held Marie's hand tight enough to squeeze the blood out. "I'm here, Mrs. Marie. I have come home to be with you."

Did Marie stir in her bed just then when Ruby spoke? Or was Ruby's her imagination wanting it to be so? Ruby poured cool water into an enamel bowl and rinsed Marie's face again and again with a cloth, trying her best to break the fever.

Ruby carefully read the doctor's instructions and took a tablespoon of the liquid to Marie every few hours, cupping a hand beneath so it wouldn't spill on her cotton nightgown. "I can't lose two mothers in one small lifetime."

For a moment, Marie opened her eyes. They were glassy and shimmered with tears, and the fever on her face made Ruby's heart ache, but she kept right on staring at Marie, willing her to live. Late that afternoon, Ruby boiled broth on the stove and then carried it up to the second floor, setting it on the dresser next to the plate of uneaten toast. "Sit up, Mrs. Marie. I have some warm soup."

Ruby tugged on Marie's arm, pulled her to a sitting position, and propped up three pillows behind her shoulders. Marie's eyes were mere slits in her face. No shimmering tears in them now. Their focus was distant as she obediently took small sips of the soup.

Hours later, Marie rested quietly, and Ruby made herself a bed on the floor to stay near. She looked out the window at a dark sky that was missing stars. "I'll be here with you all night, Mrs. Marie. I won't leave."

Several hours later, Ruby was awakened by shouting.

"Ruby? Ruby!" Marie's looked flustered and confused.

"I'm right here, Mrs. Marie." Ruby pulled the covers back up to her neck and kissed her forehead. Marie sank back into a slumber.

The next day, Mrs. Crawford stopped by to check up on them both, bringing along a basket of bread and chicken broth. Moments later, Reverend Clark stopped by to pray, his words offering hope, while Louie waited outside to be taken to school.

Mrs. Crawford remained long after he left, doing laundry and straightening the house.

"I know you want to stay here with Mrs. Bindle, but she would want you to go to school. Learning is important, especially since you want to change the world. I'll sit with her. Your school things are on the downstairs table."

"Meaning no respect, Ma Elda, but no thank you. I can't leave until Mrs. Marie is well again." Ruby crossed her arms.

"Child, you look exhausted. If you won't go to school, there's no one here who will make you. But try and get some sleep then while I look after her." When there came no reply, Ma Elda prodded, "Go on and get your rest now. You won't do anyone any good, least of all your Mrs. Marie, unless you take time to shut your eyes."

37

Morning sunlight trickled through the window and played on Marie's face, waking her up.

"Ruby, my darling dear, what are you doing here?"

Ruby awoke to see Marie's eyes open and alert. Ruby jumped up and touched Marie's brow. It was cool as the inside of an apple. A giant weight lifted from her shoulders. She sighed with relief

"How long have you been here, Ruby?"

"I came yesterday."

"What about the Crawfords? They must be upset with you." Ruby looked down at her hands. "You've cared for me by yourself?"

"The reverend came by several times to pray, and Ma Elda—I mean Mrs. Crawford—brought food and helped spell me so I could close my eyes a bit. The doctor has been here, too, twice."

"Mrs. Crawford is a good woman. I must ask her forgiveness for being so jealous of her." Marie drifted back to sleep again.

The next morning, Mrs. Crawford arrived holding a box containing all of Ruby's belongings. She put it on Ruby's bed and then checked on Marie.

Delighted to see the box, she knew the woman had given up on her. Ruby picked up her hairbrush and laid it on her dresser. She put her extra pair of shoes in the closet and was in the midst of hanging up her dresses and folding her clothes back into the drawers when she overheard Mrs. Crawford and Marie talk.

"What is Ruby doing in her room?"

"Your daughter is putting her belongings back where they belong."

"But we agreed Ruby belongs with you."

"Actually, truth be told, you agreed to my suggestion—and at a time when you were at your lowest point with your spells. I was wrong. She belongs here with you. Ruby has taught me that matters of the heart are the most important."

"Mrs. Crawford, I'm sorry."

"Ruby opened my eyes. Now must I do the same for you? When you open the front door at night and look inside, what do you see? Hopefully, a room filled with people who love one another and you, too. As for handling the gossip of people outside of the home, they just don't matter. Deal with it. Ruby has, and Ruby will be Ruby no matter what! That girl is the best medicine you can ever have. I better get going now. I'll be back tomorrow to check on you both."

Mrs. Crawford walked down the hall to say goodbye to Ruby, but before she could utter a word, Ruby grabbed hold of the woman and hugged her tightly. "Thank you. Thank you. Thank you."

The older woman cupped Ruby's face in her hands, and Ruby saw tears in her eyes.

"You'll be fine now that you've come home. If you need me for anything, come and get me. Hear?"

Ruby nodded.

The sound of the door opening and closing resonated through the house. Ruby parted the curtains and watched the fine woman walk through the yard and out the gate. Ruby turned toward Marie's room. A lot had transpired between them in the past month. It occurred to Ruby that Marie may not want her here anymore after all, and in that case, it would be best to return to the Crawfords' to live. Ruby couldn't stand it one more minute because a lifetime worth of worry stretched her to the breaking point. She scurried down the hall and then skidded to a stop just outside of Marie's door where she took a deep breath. Ruby entered the room quietly.

"That Mrs. Crawford is one exemplary woman." Marie leaned back into her bed pillows. "She made me rethink a lot of things."

"Like what?"

"Like your mother. You've never told me about her."

"I can tell you something now if you'd like." Ruby sat on a chair.

"Yes, I'd like."

"There isn't a lot I remember. She sang a lot, and she was happy, I think. I remember feeling loved. Safe."

"You've remembered the important things."

"Don't send me away again, Mrs. Marie."

"At the time, I was only thinking about what was best for you."

"Did you ever think to ask what I wanted?"

"Okay. I will ask you right now. What do you want, Ruby?"

"I want to hear Mr. Frank's stories when he gets back home from his trips. While he's gone, I want to walk barefoot along dusty roads with you. It's okay if I limp down them. I want to sit in between you and Mr. Frank at church and look up into the balcony where the negroes like me sit and wave at them. And maybe one day, some will be brave enough to come down from that balcony and sit with us on the main floor of the church. I want to say my prayers each night in my own room, not in someone's leftover room. This Christmas, I want to see an ornamented tree in the front parlor and call it the Christmas Room just for that occasion. Come spring, I want us to plant seeds on Andy's special place and think of him rolling down the hills of Heaven. That's what I want."

"Oh, Ruby, that's exactly what I want, too!" Marie sat forward and opened her arms up.

Ruby went to Marie, tripping over her heart on the way. "Am I really home?"

"Yes. You're really home for good."

Marie looked at Ruby's beaming face. Ruby's skin didn't need to be like the pale breath of winter's snow, nor Marie's skin the color of coffee for everything to be fine. Ruby made everything fine. Marie reached out and lovingly gave Ruby's hair a tug.

"I wish I could put the gold from your heart onto your skin so everyone could see your worth. While you were gone, Ruby, my heart ached so badly. Now I know God was only digging new wells inside of me to hold all the overflowing joy I've found with your return to me."

"I love you, Mrs. Marie."

"And I love you, Ruby."

"But I hear a problem in your voice."

Marie looked down and twisted a loose knot on the bedspread.

"I'm afraid for you. See, I have these awful spells at times that pull me so far down that I think I can't climb back out." Marie's arms went limp. Although fully awake, she drifted to a faraway place Ruby could not pull her from. She remembered Papa Burke getting a faraway look like that in his eyes but that was when he remembered happy thoughts; Marie was thinking terrible, sad ones. And no one could follow. Ruby would do anything to save her.

"Mrs. Marie, when you start to slide, I'll pull you back to me."

"It's good to have you back, Ruby."

38
.....
September 21, 1921

Seven in the morning, Louie sat at the table.

"It's been a week, Ruby, since we went to the police. It's time to find Grimes." Louie stuffed his mouth with the egg salad sandwiches meant for lunch.

"I'm waiting for Ma Elda. When she gets here, we can go." Ruby parted the lace curtains to look out at Marie in the backyard. Her hair fluttered in the wind, but the canvas in front of her was blank, the paint untouched.

Louie wiped his mouth with the back of his sleeve. "I thought Mrs. Bindle was well."

"The fever left her body along with the flu, but there is something in her head that vexes her spirit. "

"You need to go back to school."

"I will but not just yet."

"I can go and get Ted T. Grimes all by myself if you want to stay."

"No, I'm coming with you. Ma Elda will be here at any moment to watch Mrs. Marie for me. She thinks I'm going to school," Ruby whispered leaning over the table.

"This is the best fun yet, Ruby Red!" Louie rubbed his hands together with keenness.

"What did you tell the reverend? Lying to Ma Elda is one thing, but your dad is best friends with God, and friends stick together."

"I didn't lie. I didn't tell him a thing. It's a school day; he just thinks I'll be there."

"But isn't that still lying?" Ruby asked.

"Yeah, I guess. But you're lying then, too. Worse than me. How about if we both tell them the truth later?"

After careful consideration, Ruby replied, "Yes, I think that will work. Now quick, we need to make a list of what we need while there is still time for me to collect it all." Ruby took pencil and paper in hand and began writing, reading aloud as she wrote, "Ropes to tie him up. A flashlight in case we get back in the dark. Anything else, Louie?"

"That's it, I think. Oh wait, we need your wagon to hitch to my bike to pull Stickman back to town."

"It's in the shed behind the house."

Ruby went into the cellar to collect the items on the list as Louie got the wagon and attached it to his bike. Shortly, she returned to the table and began slipping the items into a pillow case.

"I also have a pocket knife." Louie walked back into the room. He flipped open the blade of the knife. Ruby froze in place.

"Do you think we'll really need to use that?"

"You never can tell, but I know how to use it." He closed it up and slipped it back into his pocket.

By eight, Mrs. Crawford walked through the front door like good news.

"Thank you for watching Mrs. Marie today."

"I have an uneasy feeling about today."

"Oh?" Ruby gulped.

"You've missed a week of lessons. Don't be discouraged. You have big plans for your future, and I want to see them happen."

Ruby wrapped her arms around the older woman and hugged hard. "If I could have another mama, she'd be you. I just found Mrs. Marie first."

The woman turned Ruby loose. She went outside where Marie sat in the late summer air. Ruby lingered at the backdoor and watched. "Hello, Mrs. Bindle. Marie? It's me again, Elda Crawford. I'm keeping you company for today." For a bit, Mrs. Crawford stared at the blank paper clipped to the easel, then turned her back on it before kneeling down on the grass in front of Marie. "Nice day to come back home, don't you think? Look, a blank future awaits your touch. You can paint your life any way that you want it done."

Tears crowded the corners of Ruby's eyes as she watched the tenderness coming out of Mrs. Crawford. She realized that, all her life, exemplary women had been set before her as good examples. She figured God had something to do with that.

"Ruby." Louie got impatient.

There was not another moment to waste if they were going to capture Stickman and haul him back to town before dark. Ruby pivoted and followed Louie out through the house and front door. The screen door slammed behind.

Louie walked to the bike and held onto the handles.

"You ready?"

The chilled fall air touched their cheeks. Anticipation bubbled in Ruby's belly. Up to this point, capturing Stickman had been a dream, a prayer, a mission. At this moment, it was a reality.

"Ready!" Ruby threw the pillowcase over one shoulder and rode on the fender of the bike as Louie pedaled hard. On one side of the dirt path was a field filled with grain, and on the other side, horses grazed lazily, swishing away clouds of flies that buzzed around them. Bees hummed through the wildflowers. The gray house disappeared into the distance.

The wagon kept flipping over from the bumps in the road.

"I've got an idea."

Louie jumped off his bike. He untied the rope from the wagon and pulled it down to the stream. He searched for rocks the size of his fist half-embedded in the mud at the edge of the water. Twisting them loose, little bloodsuckers scurried off from their smooth underbellies.

"Want one of these for a new pet?"

"Ewww!"

"Ewww? This comes from someone who kept a cockroach as a pet?"

One by one, they pulled up rocks and then put them into the wagon. The weight held the wagon on course. Just as they readied to cross to the other side at the stream's shallows, Ruby's heart began to beat hard against her chest. Through the gray morning fog ran a thread of sunlight that swirled down to the earth. In the center, sat a black woman in a pale red dress wearing a straw hat.

"Mother?" she softly whispered. "Stop, Louie, stop! I see my mother."

Louie pressed on the brakes, tipping the bike over. They both fell to the ground.

"What is it, Ruby?" Louie brushed dirt from his trousers.

"Look! It's— it's— That's my *mother!*" She ran down to the stream and spun around. The woman had disappeared.

"There's no one there." He guffawed.

"I thought I saw her. Right here."

"Oh, Ruby. You have such an imagination." Louie shook his head. "Come on, we have important business, remember?"

"I've been trying to find my mother since I was five."

"Maybe this is your moment of decision."

"What do you mean?" Ruby set her hands on her hips.

"Do you want to keep looking for what you lost or enjoy what's right in front of you? Ruby, time's wasting. Decide here and now."

Ruby stared at the stream completely bathed in sunlight. It was so bright she had to close her eyes. She saw her mother slipping through the crowd, relived the piercing terror of that moment. Then felt the warm hand of Mama Burke upon finding her. How safe she felt when Papa Burke dried her eyes. In her cluttered thoughts, she saw Myna scrubbing pots while talking about prayers. She giggled, recalling Marie opening up all the cabinets and ice box, telling her to eat anything she wanted. As she opened her eyes, Frank's laughter came to her on the breeze. And finally, Ma Elda's tears flowed in the stream.

"I'm ready. Let's go."

Crossing the stream at the shallows, they headed into woods. The road became so narrow and steep that they dismounted and pushed the bike and wagon along.

"See the back of that boulder? The old shack is just on the other side. Stickman is hiding there. I tell you, it's his hide-out." Louie puffed hard.

"It'll be difficult for me to get to." Ruby looked at the rocky hillside. Her knees shook from the physical struggle. Louie was good to lean on.

"I don't mind telling you, Ruby: I'm feeling a bit scared."

"Well, stop it!" She shoved him hard.

"Hey, what was that for?"

"Don't go soft on me. Just keep thinking about the reward money. I might have a good idea for it."

They left the bike and wagon there and continued on without them.

Another few feet and they spotted the shanty.

"Didn't you say he lived in a shack?" Ruby asked with surprise.

"Yeah, in the daylight, it looks different." Louie scratched his head.

"Looks like a lean-to. Marie has one in the back of our house for her paints." Ruby walked closer. "I don't think anyone lives here. You're wrong, Louie."

A deep voice startled them from behind. "What do you kids want?"

39

There stood the infamous Ted T. Grimes with a large knife in his hand.

"Can I help you two with something?" he asked.

"Umm." Louie's eyes darted around. He seemed nervous. "Just out for a walk."

"This is my woods. You're trespassing."

"Who says these woods belong to you?" Ruby asked.

"I say so. Go on, get home!" He looked tired and thin. He was a mean-looking man with heavy lines near his mouth that said he did a lot of frowning.

"Sure, we'll get on home now." Louie grinned and walked away, pulling Ruby along.

Ruby scowled.

As soon as they were out of earshot, Ruby let him have it. "Are you crazy? What were you thinking? We need to get Stickman." Ruby clenched her fist.

"Hold on," Louie said, smiling. "Didn't you see that large knife? It's bigger than mine. We had a plan to get here. But we didn't have a plan on how to capture him. For now, let's follow him."

"Okay. That's more like it."

"You need to trust me more. It hurts my feelings when you don't." Louie attempted to keep a straight face, but one corner of his mouth kept trying to grin.

Hiding behind a bush with the pillowcase in hand, they watched the Stickman enjoy his lunch of roasted squirrel. With a rumbling stomach, Ruby remembered Louie's egg salad sandwiches.

"Hand me the rope. Stay here till I call you out, understand?" Louie said.

Ruby ducked behind a boulder. "Keep your knife handy."

Louie stood up and walked to the campfire, swinging the rope easily in his hand. On the way, he tripped over it and fell on the ground. Ted T. Grimes looked startled.

"What you want boy? I told you and that girl to get on home!"

"That's just the problem. I lost her! She ran away from her folks, and they paid me ten cents to get her back for them. I should've used this rope they gave me to tie her up, but I'm not sure how to do that."

"What do you mean?" Grimes pulled the fully cooked squirrel from the fire and tore off one of the legs. He shoved it into his mouth and a bit of burned flesh hung over his lower lip.

"Which end of this do you use to tie her up with?" Louie asked looking confused.

Grimes laughed and hit his knee. "You sure ain't a smart one, are you?"

Louie just grinned. "Can you show me how to tie a person?"

"Sure," Grimes answered. He reached for the rope. With

great care he tied Louie's wrists together and pulled it tight all while explaining how it was done. Ruby peeked out.

"Wow! That was good, Mister, but I'm a slow learner—can't even read. My teacher says I need to practice things a while before I know how to do it. Mind if I practice on you?"

"I don't know about that," he answered, untying the boy.

"My knots are always too loose and people just slip right out of them. I think you're probably stronger than she is, so if you can't get out of them, then I know she can't either. I mean, it is ten cents," Louie said.

"Oh, alright. Go ahead and tie my wrists." Grimes held out his wrists to Louie who was now free from the rope.

Louie studied the rope as if he had never held one before this day. Grimes held his wrists out closer to Louie like a patient schoolmaster.

"Yup, yup, doing it right," Grimes told him as the ropes began to circle his wrists. "I think you learn fast, boy!" After Louie tied him off tightly, Grimes twisted his arms and wrists every which way but could not budge them. "No one can get out of these."

"Suppose I get her hands tied and she kicks me with her feet? What do I do then, Mister?" Louie held up the other end of the rope and wagged it as a dog's tail.

"You hog-tie her, boy. I'll tell you how that is done."

"Gee, thanks, Mister."

Grimes lay on the ground on his belly while Louie wrapped the rope around and around his legs and tied them tight.

"Done good. Now cut me loose, and you can go on your way."

"You sure ain't a smart one, are you? Come on out now, Ruby!" Louie called.

Ruby ran out pulling the wagon along.

"Why you awful kids! Untie me right now! Or I'll—"

"I don't think you'll be doing much of anything, Mr. Ted T. Grimes," Ruby said, picking up his knife from near the fire and handing it to Louie.

"What— Are you that little girl from the train station?"

"That's right. And you're the terrible man who beat an orphan boy to death!"

"And now we're taking you to the police," Louie said, puffing out his chest. After dumping out the river rocks, together, they got the man into the wagon. He hung over the end of it by two feet.

It was hard pulling the wagon along the dirt path. Sticks and rocks kept getting in the way, jamming the wheels. Finally, they decided to leave the bike and come back for it later. It took both of them to haul the heavy wagon.

The growing dark didn't help, but they were determined and forged ahead. Further trouble soon came in the form of rain. Along the edge of an incline, they pushed the wagon, and Stickman fought to free himself of the ropes until Louie brandished the large knife.

"If I have to, I'll use this on you." Stickman must have believed him because he remained still and silent the rest of the way into town.

They heard a welcome noise coming towards them in the darkness. Water spilled over rocks. The stream was just ahead. They could follow it home. Ruby turned on the flashlight to help find their way. Into the shallows, they tugged the wagon. Wading across to the opposite side, the wagon tipped several times, dumping Grimes into the cold water. It took all their strength to get the man back inside of it. Up on the other side, they pulled him in the wagon. Ruby's feet went deep into mud, and she fell. She lost one of her shoes and spent minutes digging through sludge to find it. Meanwhile, gusts of wind-blown rain pummeled them. Finally, she gave up. Ruby's legs hurt up to her eyeballs.

"I don't feel so good."

"Almost there," Louie said. "Just keep moving."

Soon, they saw the lights of Denton through the drizzling rain. Ruby pulled the crumpled wanted poster from her pocket and pinned it to Stickman's shirt.

"No mistaking him now!"

40

They were within blocks of the police station. The closer they got, the busier the sidewalks got with folks.

"Is there a carnival in town?" Ruby asked.

"Not that I know of." Louie looked around. Whatever the occasion, they seemed to be in the middle of it.

"Hey, are they the missing children?" someone asked.

"I think they are!" another answered.

"Are you the missing children?" someone else asked them.

"What are they talking about, Louie? We aren't missing. Who's missing?"

Then they heard applause and shouts of congratulations. Folks walked next to them, and whistles blew. Laughter rose in great waves.

"It's the missing children, and look who they have!" a woman shouted. "The most wanted man in Denton."

"Someone run to the station and get the police," a man yelled.

"Do you need help with that load?" another man asked.

"We found him. We'll take him ourselves." Louie was firm.

In front of the police station waited two anxious fathers.

The two young adventurers stopped in front of Mr. Frank and Reverend Clark. Ruby looked at them as if she had been lost in the rain all her life. Her dress was torn and clung to her, and by now both shoes were gone. She felt trapped—like a fly in a teacup—as she waited for him with her eyes. The momentary silence stuffed her ears. Then she saw it. Love crept behind his eyes, and his face lit up with relief.

"Ruby! We've been so worried about you and Louie. Where have you been?"

"Mr. Frank! You're home!" Ruby dropped the handle of the wagon and ran to him. "We've been on police business and captured Grimes."

"You two shouldn't have gone. Capturing wanted men is police work," Reverend Clark said.

"We tried to tell the police, but no one listened, so we went ourselves." Louie sounded proud. "We found him hiding a ways from here in a cave."

"You two mix like gasoline and a bonfire," Frank said.

"I'm so glad you're back," Ruby said. "Mrs. Marie has been so sick. It's too hard for me to manage her and school all alone. We need you."

"I'm here now to take care of both of you."

The desk police officer walked out to see what the commotion was all about and burst into laughter at the sight of them. Patting Frank on the back, he declared, "That girl of yours looks like a delicate flower, but she's tough as nails!"

"Yup, she's my girl alright," Frank smiled at Ruby.

The policeman turned on his heels and yelled for help to carry Ted T. Grimes into a cell. Then he put his hand on Louie's head. "You get a reward for bringing him in, son. The reward is a hundred dollars."

"Wait a minute! The poster said it's *five* hundred dollars," Louie corrected. "And Ruby and I both—"

"You did a good job, Louie. I just helped pull. The five hundred dollars will go a long way to adding on the church addition."

"Church addition?" Louie crowed.

"Just think of all the good it'll do," Ruby urged. "Besides, everything you need, you already have: a mom and dad who love you, a roof over your head, food, and clothes. There's nothing left to want."

"Yeah, I guess you're right," Louie reluctantly agreed.

Reverend Clark beamed, "Louie, what a generous gift!"

"Goodnight, all." Ruby smiled and hooked her arm through Frank's. Behind her she heard the crowd cheering Louie.

Frank and Ruby rode home together in the darkness. They didn't have any more words to say to each other. They felt comfortable sitting side by side, going home to where they belonged together. Marie and Frank would take care of her.

When they arrived, Ruby smelled dinner. Lifting the lid on the roaster, she noticed only the edges of the roast had burned. A warm dinner would sure taste good tonight. She looked questioningly at Frank. Then, as if to answer her silent question, Marie stepped into the room.

"Ruby, there you are. I've been looking all over for you."

"Here I am, Mrs. Marie."

"Frank arrived this morning just minutes after you left. We walked to meet you after school, and the teacher told us she hadn't seen you in weeks! If I'd lost you because of my—"

Ruby dashed into Marie's arms and hugged her tight. It was as if Marie had gotten strong and all healed up in the singleness of one day. And on the dining room table was a new painting. It was the most beautiful one yet.

They ate dinner on the front porch, their plates piled with slices of roast and bread smeared with slabs of butter. The wind had turned and now blew from the southwest as it cleared away the clouds and rain. Stars blinked into view above them. Ruby thought of Andy winking friendly eyes at them.

That night in bed, Ruby went over the day's events in her head. She felt refreshed having let go of the past. She was ready for the future. She thought of Louie and how scared they both had been. Perhaps bravery didn't lie in being fearless but in proceeding despite fear. She yawned and stretched her legs out to get rid of the soreness in them. Then she fell asleep to the sounds of the typewriter and the smell of fresh turpentine.

41
....
Christmas, 1921

"Hurry, Ruby! The Crawfords will be here soon," Marie called up the stairwell. She held a plate of Christmas cookies.

"Coming, Mom!" Ruby hurried down the steps wearing a bright red velvet dress with a plaid apron, both trimmed with lace.

"You look lovely!" Frank spun her around.

"Thanks, Dad. And thank you for my new shoes, too."

"My pleasure." He beamed.

Ruby walked into the Christmas Room. The long needle pine tree, freshly cut a week earlier, stood at the front window. At the time, Marie had taken down a box from the attic that held family heirloom glass ornaments from Italy wrapped in cotton. The green and red garland they cut from construction paper to wind around the tree, top to bottom. Electric bubble lights gave the tree a whimsical appearance, creating dancing figures on the walls. On top of the tree was a star that Ruby had made at school out of cardboard and silver glass glitter. Marie had suggested peppermint candy canes, but Ruby had lost her taste for them while still back in New York. Her life was moving forward, leaving former things behind.

"I so love our tree, and oh, the Christmas Room is beautiful." Ruby twirled about, feeling free and welcome to be here, basking in the beauty.

"Look, Ruby. Your stocking is filled already. I even made one for Joel and one for James." Marie pointed at the fireplace.

"What did you slip inside?"

"An apple, a handful of walnuts, a bird whistle, and a Gyroscope Top. There's even a stocking for Andy."

Tears welled in Ruby's eyes. "He would have loved it here."

Marie reached for Ruby's hand and gave it a comforting squeeze. "It's the letting go that's so difficult."

Ruby looked into Andy's stocking. "Andy's stocking is empty."

"I thought we'd fill it later, together."

"With what?"

"With thoughts of him. Memories. All written down. Next year, we'll take them out when the stockings are hung and read them again."

"And we will never forget."

"Never," Marie agreed.

"Even though Marie and I knew and loved him for just a short time, we still think of him and will continue to do so until there are no more thoughts or ties of earth left inside to keep us here," Frank said.

"Andy brought you home to us, Ruby."

The doorbell rang and in came the Crawford family with delightful food dishes: a fat ham, stuffed acorn squash, sausage stuffing, fresh cranberry orange relish, glazed carrots, Christmas Flat Cake, and five pumpkin pies.

"Does there happen to be a mincemeat pie among this food?" Ruby asked.

"Oh dear, no. Why? Did you want one?" Mrs. Crawford asked.

"No, never mind." Ruby smiled.

"You are so kind to bring all this food," Marie gushed as she helped carry the food to the dining room's sideboard.

"I love cooking and wanted to bring all our favorites. And look at your dishes. Tell me about them."

"Antipasto salad with dressing, maple-candied yams, three kinds of sweet rolls. Oh, and Ruby contributed the Christmas cookies."

They prayed holding hands and spoke of wishes for the New Year.

"Come spring, I'm gonna teach myself to drive Dad's truck."

"*I* will teach you to drive my truck." Frank nudged her leg with his.

"Even better!" Marie laughed.

Ruby took a long look at Marie, trying to find a smidge of her falling apart at the seams, but all she saw was health and rosy cheeks. She allowed herself to take a deep break and relax.

"What did Santa bring you for Christmas morning?" Mrs. Crawford asked sipping punch.

"An easel of my very own." Ruby beamed.

"The perfect gift for you." Mrs. Crawford continued, "And what have you given your parents?"

Ruby smiled shyly and said, "They'll get it later tonight. But I have a gift for you, Ma Elda." By now, Ruby had fused her name into something which sounded more like Melda. Ruby excused herself from the table and returned with a gift. "It's for you, too, Mr. Crawford."

Mrs. Crawford pulled the paper from around the canvas. It was a drawing of her baking cakes in the kitchen while Ford read the newspaper. "Oh, Ruby. This is really beautiful! I shall always treasure it."

After supper was cleaned up and put away, they waved goodbye to the Crawfords and returned to the Christmas Room to enjoy the last few hours left in the day. Ruby pulled a small gift she had hidden at the back of the tree and handed it to Marie and Frank. They unwrapped it carefully. It was a wooden heart painted red. A wire was attached at the top.

"Ruby, this is great. A good gift."

"I couldn't want anything more. Look, I can hang it on the front door." Marie held it up.

"In school, we're learning about symbols. This heart symbolizes how I feel about you. I've given you both my heart."

"And you have ours," Marie said, and Frank nodded his agreement.

"We have one more gift for you." Marie went to the desk and retrieved a paper which she handed to Frank.

"We've applied to the state for a name change for you, if you want it."

"You don't like the name Ruby?"

"We like both your names, Ruby Red. But the change would be to add a name to the end. Bindle. The adoption has finally gone through."

Ruby gasped.

"But only if you want that name."
"But what about what people will say?"
"We don't care about that anymore, Ruby, unless you do," Marie said.
"Then my answer is, yes. Yes, I want your name." Ruby threw her arms around them and looked at the Christmas tree. "I have one more wish."

With blankets underneath for comfort and over them for warmth, they snuggled in their nightgowns and nightshirts beneath the lighted tree in the Christmas Room.

Ruby looked up through the limbs of the tree at the sparkly lights and the glass ornaments that came all the way from Italy. Marie talked about how her grandmother brought them with her on her voyage to America 50 years ago.

"Did they have children?" Ruby asked.

"After Nonna and Nonno arrived in America, they bought their own bakery in New York. And they had one girl: my mother."

"Did she ever leave you?"

"No, never. She died a few years ago, when my spells first began. Then I met Frank, and I came to Texas with him."

"Mr. Frank, why were you in New York City?"

"I was running a story about the Orphan Train for my newspaper. I went to this wonderful bakery with delicious desserts. And there was Marie, standing behind the counter with flour in her hair." He laughed along with Marie. "When she agreed to be my wife, we came back to Texas."

"And then you met the Orphan Train when it came to Denton with me on board."

"That was my follow up a few years later. A wonderful ending to an exciting beginning."

"Yes, because I was on it." Ruby yawned. She was exhausted but felt happy wrapped up in these stories. Family stories. Her stories now.

"Frank, did you know we have a daughter who plans on being an advocate for civil rights?"

"I've heard our daughter talk about it. A lot."

"These are good times to be living in. You'll grow to be a strong woman, Ruby."

"I wonder if my mother was a strong woman."

"She was strong. And kind. And charitable." Marie smiled.

"How do you know that?"

Marie turned to face Ruby. "Because I know her daughter."

She looked into Marie's violet eyes, the color of evening skies.

"I know I was put on this earth to love Frank and to love you," Marie said.

"And I was put on earth to love you right back!" Ruby hugged them both.

It seemed to Ruby that things were finally where they were meant to be all along. She threaded her fingers through Frank's and Marie's and recited a poem:

> *She wandered in the wilderness.*
> *And then a door opened*
> *for the black girl who roamed.*
> *They saw no difference,*
> *not the white man or the olive lady,*
> *And gave me a place called home.*

Marie beamed. "That's beautiful. Which poet wrote that?"
"Ruby Red Bindle."
Ruby held Marie's hand against her face. Frank said goodnight prayers with them. And beneath the tree in the Christmas Room, they slept.

Come summer, the garden would be adorned with butterflies and honeysuckle vines. The air thick with the scent of blossoming prairie flowers stretching from their front door to where Andy now rested in peace.

Ruby loved the gray shuttered house because, apart from being old and cluttered, it held the imagination of Frank, who came and went, and the essence of Marie, whose mind and mood played tricks on her from time to time. They were three people who loved one another, and Ruby never minded when they got in one another's way. Ruby rose at eight to get her chores done except for the days she got up at seven for school. On Sundays, they lunched at two while she and Marie communed over the rich colors of the seasons—and Frank typed his stories on his typewriter. It was more than enough to be happy.

THE END

Acknowledgements

Special recognition to Reverend Christy Thomas for her tenacity and insightfulness which continually inspires.

Gratefulness to Elise Matthews whose diligent editing and suggestions turn to gold.

Talented Amy Munoz, thank you for the incredibly creative book cover.

To Dot Thompson for open doors. Ruby and I have found a good friend in you.

Special mention to Donna Henry.

Discussion Questions

Which facet of Ruby's character is most admirable and why?

How does the setting of the story help the plot move forward?

Why did people take in children from The Orphan Train?

Compare and contrast Marie and Frank.

Describe Ruby's conflict at the start of the book. How does the conflict change by the end?

How would you have handled being tossed out in winter with no place to go?

What does Andy's butterfly fly theory have to do with Ruby?

Explain Ruby's and Andy's relationship.

Explain Ruby's relationship with Louie and how it changes throughout the story.

Pick one of the main characters to journal about.

Marie's last picture was beautiful. The author doesn't tell us what it looked like. Either describe or draw when you think it looks like.

Explain the significant of the Orphan Train in the early 1900s.

Red had a significant impact on Ruby. Explain.

Write a character sketch of Ruby.

Name three events that made Ruby indomitable.

Explain how Marie's paintings change with how she's feeling.

About the Author

Robin Jansen is an educator with four teaching certificates and over 30 years of classroom experience. During the day, she is the Special Education Coordinator, ESL Director, GED Advisor, and State Testing Coordinator at the Denton County Juvenile Justice System for at-risk students. By night, she is an avid reader and compulsive writer. Robin has two grown children and two grandsons. She resides in Denton with her rescue animals.

Robin Jansen also writes under the name Robin Shope. This is her eleventh book. Her stories have also appeared in various short story collections.

Also by the Author

Revell (Baker Publishing Group)
    The Chase
    The Replacement
    The Candidate

White Rose Press (Pelican Book Group)
    Journey to Paradise, The Christmas Edition
    The Valentine Edition
    The Easter Edition
    Wynn in the Willows

The Wild Rose Press
    WildCard
    The Debutante Murders (trilogy)

Downtown Girl Press
    Passages

PAX TV produced one of her short stories, "Mom's Last Laugh."

The Christmas Edition is a feature film on DVD.

Enthuse Entertainment has acquired rights to The Chase.

CPSIA information can be obtained
at www.ICGtesting.com
Printed in the USA
FSOW02n1721031116
26876FS